The Xandra: Book 2
Mother of Light

By
Herbert Grosshans

Published by
Melange Books, LLC
White Bear Lake, MN 55110
www.melange-books.com

ISBN 978-1-61235-012-7
Mother of Light, The Xandra Book 2 Copyright © 2006, 2011
Herbert Grosshans

Credits

Cover Artist: A. Bratt
Editor: Taylor Evans
Copy Editor: Mae Powers
Format: Mae Powers

The Xandra: Book 2
Mother of Light
By Herbert Grosshans

Needing to escape the alien Xandra, Commander Beringer and his 27 marines went into cryogenic suspension, hoping to find safety in the future.

One thousand years later they are awakened from their deep sleep and are anxious to find out what happened…

You can visit Herbert at his blog
http://www.hegro.blogspot.com

The Xandra Trilogy
Seeds of Chaos Book 1 Eden's Gate
Seeds Of Chaos Book 2 Hell's Gate
Stardogs, Book One, Return to Redsky
Stardogs, Book Two, Redemption
Orion—The Hunt
Cliffs of Time

The Xandra: Book 2
Mother of Light
By Herbert Grosshans

Prologue

When one of Earth's Exploration ships, carrying colonists sleeping in cryogenic suspension, found a planet suitable for colonization they named it Nu-Eden. One thousand colonists were transported down to the planet's surface to start populating their new found paradise, but they soon discovered they were not alone. A sentient being who calls herself 'The Xandra' slowly absorbed the colonists and replaced them with identical duplicates.

The Xandra managed to invade the alien space station, which is circling Nu-Eden, and she replaced the 197 human observers who were on board of the station. Only Commander Beringer and his 27 marines managed to escape and find refuge with the alien Genaar, deep inside the huge space station. They went into cryogenic suspension, hoping to find safety in the future.

One thousand years later they are awakened from their deep sleep and are anxious to find out what happened…

Chapter One

The roar of a swamp-tiger interrupted the silence of the dark forest. Viran glanced at the team leader. He showed signs of wariness. Horgan was getting too old for these gathering missions. He should never have come on this one. Time for a younger man to take charge.

Rah and Roh, the two sky-wanderers, already appeared in the evening sky. Their silvery bright light began to illuminate the dark interior of the forest. Viran did not fear the wanderers, but he feared the night creatures they awakened.

The sea would become too choppy for the ship to begin the return journey to their island. They would have to spend the night hidden among the rocks on the seashore.

"How long?" He asked the team leader.

Horgan shifted his axe from one big-knuckled hand to the other and shrugged his massive shoulders. "Not long," he growled.

"I hear the Tree-devils above us," said Rim, one of the young warriors. He held his spear awkwardly in his big hands.

"The Tree-devils are harmless," Horgan said. "It's the Neanders I worry about."

Viran had never seen one of those big hairy brutes that roamed the forest at night, but according to the stories they were twice a man's height and solid muscles, their bodies covered with long shaggy hair, and their mouths so big, they could swallow a child with one bite.

Viran shuddered and gripped his war-hammer tighter. He would not give up without a fight. He would smash at least one shaggy skull.

"This load is beginning to get heavy," a voice said behind him. Viran looked back at Deter, who staggered under the weight of the big basket full of herbs he had strapped to his broad back. Roc and Raul walked close behind Deter, equally loaded up.

All three youths were big and strong, chosen for missions like this one, but they had been traveling far too long and it began to show in their movements.

Hager, who brought up the rear, called out suddenly, "We have company!"

They must have been hiding in the trees, waiting silently for the Humans to walk into their trap. Neanders were not too smart, but they were cunning. At least a dozen of them dropped into their midst.

Viran swung his big hammer and smashed it onto a shaggy head. He uttered a triumphant war cry as his opponent crumbled to the ground. Beside him Rim pulled his bloodied spear out of a thick, hairy body.

Another huge shadow loomed in front of Viran, long sharp teeth gleamed in a gaping mouth. Viran didn't have enough time to raise his hammer; he just lifted it, pushed it forward into the ugly face and registered the cracking of bones with grim satisfaction.

An angry roar erupted beside him. Pulling back his hammer, he drove the wooden handle into another of the creatures. He heard the dull thud of the impact, and then a pair of muscular hairy arms wrapped themselves around his chest in a crushing grip. He almost gagged when the stench of the Neander rose up into his nostrils. His arms pinned to his sides, he couldn't lift his weapon. Even though big and strong, Viran felt helpless in the embrace of the big brute. Twisting and thrashing, he tried to dislodge the creature. When he thought his ribs would crack, the pressure suddenly lifted and he slipped out of the deadly embrace. He looked up to see Horgan grinning at him, his axe still embedded in the hairy back of the Neander.

"You've done well, all of you," Horgan said.

Viran became aware of the sudden silence and realized the fight was over. He stared down at the lifeless bodies of their attackers. "They are not as large as I was made to believe," he said.

"They are big enough," Hager said, wiping the sharp blade of his spear tip on the shaggy coat of one of the Neanders. "That last one almost got you, Viran."

"I know, but thanks to Horgan's mighty axe I am alive." He took a few deep breaths, winced when pain from bruised ribs shot through his body. Picking up his war-hammer, which had dropped from powerless fingers, he looked at Horgan. "You saved my life, I won't forget," he said.

Horgan laughed. "You would have done the same for me." He looked at the others. "I am proud of you. You're a good team." His eyes fixed on Rim, who nursed his left arm where a sharp claw had left an ugly red mark. "You've been bloodied today, now you are a real man, young Rim."

"More company," Hager cried out and brought up his spear.

A shadowy figure dropped from the branches, then three more. Tree-devils. Small humanoid creatures with large, black eyes.

Viran rushed to his companion's aid, swinging his heavy hammer. This puzzled him. Tree-devils never attacked Humans.

"Don't harm them!" Horgan bellowed. He shouldered his beefy body past Viran. "I know what they want. We are being summoned."

"Summoned?" Viran asked. "What do you mean by that?"

"The Xandra needs our services," the older man said and a sly grin split his craggy features. "It is an experience you won't forget as long as you live."

"How do you know?" Hager demanded. Young, tall and lanky, he didn't look much of a warrior, but he threw a spear with better accuracy than most.

"It happened to me when I was young," Horgan explained, "relax, we are in no danger."

"I don't trust these ugly creatures," Rim said, pointing his spear at one of them.

The little creature stared at him with his large round eyes, then it turned and began walking back on the narrow path. The other three followed him. One looked back at the Humans, lifted a long arm and made a beckoning gesture.

"We better follow," Horgan said.

"I don't like it." Viran looked at the others.

"Neither do I." Raul said. "What about our packs? I can't carry mine much further."

"Leave them. We'll pick them up again when we come back." Horgan turned to follow the Tree-devils.

"*If* we come back," Hager snorted.

"We will, now let's go."

Muttering, they dropped their baskets and, reluctantly, they followed their leader. They didn't worry too much about the contents of their baskets. The herbs and berries would keep. The baskets were woven from tough vines and covered with thick skins taken from sea bulls.

As they walked behind the four small creatures Viran heard twittering voices and soft rustling in the branches above. When he looked up, he saw small dark shadows flitting through the trees.

They hadn't walked long when they came to a fork in the path, one of many Viran remembered seeing when they came this way before. The *Tree-devils* took the narrower path, and they followed it for quite some time.

"I don't have a good feeling about this," said Raul, as he walked behind Viran. "I wish I had a better weapon than just my knife."

"You won't need a weapon," Horgan rumbled and laughed.

"What's funny?" Raul demanded to know.

"You'll see." The big man chuckled to himself. "You'll see."

The path became wider, ended in a clearing. Before them lay the ruins of some kind of building. Moss covered the wide steps that led to a gaping opening. Creeping vines clung to crumbling pillars and rough stone walls. The two moons threw double shadows as they bathed the ancient ruins with their silvery light.

"What is this place?" Rim, the youngest of the team, asked.

"It's a place of worship," said Horgan. "Look at those statues!" He pointed to a row of weathered stone carvings, all of them representation of the female form, in different poses. "This is where they worship the Mother of Light."

"Pretty gloomy place," murmured Raul, "gives me the shivers."

Viran realized suddenly that the Tree-devils were gone. "Now what?" he asked Horgan.

The team leader stared at the dark opening that led into the interior of the ancient building. "We'll go inside," he said.

Gripping his war-hammer tight in his right fist, Viran followed the big man. The others tagged along with little enthusiasm.

As their eyes adjusted to the darkness inside, they saw a large chamber. Moonlight spilled through openings in the slime covered stone walls. As if by design the light illuminated a chair carved from stone in the center of the chamber.

The chair was occupied.

At first Viran mistook it for another statue, but then the figure moved and rose. Viran gasped. He'd never seen a woman of such beauty before.

Tall, her red, flaming hair falling across bare shoulders and spilling down her back, her breasts large and round, and her legs long and slim, she looked like a vision out of a dream.

She stepped fully into the moonlight, and Viran moaned when he saw her perfect naked body and her beautiful face.

"I am The Xandra," she said in a clear, but seductive, throaty voice. "Welcome to my temple."

"She's not real," whispered Roc who stood beside Viran. "No woman can be that beautiful."

"I am real," said the Xandra, "but I am no mortal woman. I am The Mother of Light. I am a goddess."

"What do you want from us?" Horgan asked boldly.

The woman laughed. "You know what I want, Horgan. We have met before, when you were young."

"How do you know?"

"I am a goddess. I never forget, but I also see it in your mind. I see that you haven't forgotten either, that all your life you've ached for the time you spent in my embrace."

"It is not you who I remember," Horgan said.

She laughed again. "I was the one. I appear in many forms." She paused and sighed. "This temple used to be a thing of beauty and splendor. Now it is rotting away, covered with mold and dust, home to fire-lizards and dust-vipers." She lifted a slim arm. "My angels will guide you to a place that is more suitable."

A shadow obscured the moonlight coming through the window. When Viran looked he saw the silhouette of a slim creature outlined against the sky. Silvery wings glittered in the moonlight as the angel fluttered gracefully to the ground.

Another one appeared, then two more.

The first one landed in front of the Humans, and Viran stared at the slim, naked winged girl. She was exquisitely formed, her breasts small, but firm, and her face so lovely he ached when he looked at it. Fine golden hair cascaded in soft curls down to her buttocks. Viran looked into her eyes. They were large and as blue as the sky on a cloudless day. She smiled, and his heart melted.

"I am Angela," she said with a clear, but somewhat childish voice. "Come." She folded her silvery wings and walked on small, delicate feet.

The other three angels were just as naked, just as lovely.

The men followed them outside, down the moss-covered steps. They entered a narrow path, which they walked for awhile. It led them into a large clearing, with a pond in the middle. On its placid water floated a giant plant. It appeared round and thick, its surface covered with soft, purple petals.

A group of young girls were bathing in the water. A few sat on rocks beside the pond, all of them beautiful and naked. Viran never saw so many lovely breasts and bare round buttocks before.

The men stopped at the edge of the clearing and just stared at those naked female bodies. Three of the winged girls spread their wings and lifted into the air. The remaining one looked at Viran. "The Mother has chosen you," she said with her childlike voice.

"Chosen for what?" Viran asked and touched her gently on the shoulder. "You are very lovely," he said without waiting for her answer.

She smiled.

His hand moved down to her breast, cupped it. She removed it with a gentle hand. "I cannot give you what you seek," she said.

"Is it forbidden?"

"Not forbidden." She smiled. "It is not possible." She took his hand, guided it between her legs. His fingers encountered nothing but smooth, soft skin.

"I am forever a virgin," she said. She looked at him sadly and added, "by design. The pleasures of the flesh are denied me." Her lips touched his fleetingly, then she opened her wings and took to the air. She hovered in front of him for a moment. "I have no such desires," she said, rose into the night sky and disappeared above the trees.

Chapter Two

Viran watched the winged girl fly away. How did such beings come into existence? They had no means of propagating. Such beauty-- wasted! Shaking his head, he took a deep breath and became aware of the sweet musky odor in the crisp night-air. Above him, the two wanderers were nearing each other, soon they'd be touching. The sea would be rough by now, but their ship was safely anchored in the quiet bay. The guards left behind probably worried and wondered what happened to them, especially Old Grisgaar.

Viran smiled, thinking of the many nights spent listening to the exploits of the old grisly warrior.

The soft touch of a warm hand on his arm made him turn. One of the girls from the lake stood in front of him, water still dripping from her naked body. When he looked into her large violet eyes he forgot about the winged girl. Her long black hair hung loosely down her back. He stared at her large and somewhat conical shaped breasts and let his gaze linger on the sparse black hair covering her pubic area. Viran felt his penis thicken and rise between his legs. It pressed painfully against the leather breeches he wore.

The girl smiled, lifted up on her toes and put her soft lips against his. She tasted sweet, and when she parted her lips her tongue darted against his teeth. Opening his mouth, he sucked on her tongue and swallowed the sweet nectar that flowed from it. Her hands went down to his belt, opened it, and then her warm fingers circled around his manhood.

He moaned and put his big hands on her smooth, full buttocks, pulling her against him. No girl had ever done this to him. The girls of his tribe were not this bold and none of them this beautiful.

Life on the island was harsh. Children grew up fast. Girls became old women before their time, and boys became men as soon as they reached puberty. Women of his tribe needed to earn their place in the community as much as a man needed to. They didn't have the luxury to play and relax. Most of their time they spent just to survive.

Viran remembered copulating with Gerilda, a girl a little older, big and strong like a man, and coupling with her had been rough and furious. A couple of other girls, Sinda and Nelly, proved not much different.

Now here he encountered this fragile girl with a smile so sweet and warm it could melt the rocks by the seashore, and her touch so soft that it filled his body with strange desires and made his belly ache.

She pushed down his breeches and freed his manhood. Then she slid down in front of him, let her tongue glide over his chest, his belly, down to his groin. He groaned when her warm lips kissed his straining member, and then he cried out hoarsely as she sucked it deep into her mouth.

The pleasure seemed unbearable. His penis throbbed inside her warm mouth, but before he exploded she pulled away. She lay down on her back and looked up at him expectantly.

His eyes riveted on her open thighs, they saw the pink slit underneath soft, silky black curls. He stepped out of his breeches and fell to his knees between her spread thighs. Running his hands over her flat belly, he let his fingers describe circles around her genitals. Then he bent down, put his tongue into her slit and licked it gently.

He swallowed, drank from her flowing fountain. Liquid fire ran down his throat. His rod felt like a piece of rockwood between his legs.

The girl put her hands on his head. He looked up, saw her smile. He stretched out on top of her, guided his hard member, and with a mighty thrust he entered her deeply.

She writhed underneath him with snakelike motions, met his thrusts, but she was eerily silent, never uttered a sound.

It didn't matter. He howled like a wild creature of the night when he erupted inside her.

She pushed him off, even though he could have continued. Watching her as she ran to the water, he admired her slim form, her plump buttocks, and the way her long hair fluttered in the slight breeze.

She disappeared in the water.

When Viran looked around, he saw Horgan lying on his back, a young girl bouncing fiercely on top of him and another one straddling his head. Viran saw the big man's mouth glued to the girl's genitals.

Young Rim knelt behind another girl, his big hands around her slim hips. His buttocks clenched every time he thrust forward, while his lean loins slammed into the girl's soft round buttocks.

The others were similarly engaged with the girls from the pond.

A girl emerged out of the water. She came toward Viran. When she came close she smiled and took his hand and pulled him into the path that led back to the temple.

"Where are we going?" Viran asked, but the girl said nothing, just smiled at him.

Viran still sprouted an erection. The touch of the girl's hand in his made it worse, he desired her more than anything else right now. He watched her breasts bounce up and down as she moved gracefully, slightly ahead of him. Her thick black hair, still wet from the water, reflected the moonlight. He looked at the play of her small, but fleshy buttocks and felt the urge so strong in him that he had to force his eyes away from her.

His gaze moved to the sky. Through the thick tree branches he saw that Rah and Roh as one now.

He shuddered.

When the two wanderers became lovers, things were not always what they seemed.

The temple loomed darkly ahead. The girl pulled him up the ancient steps, his bare feet crushed soft moss underneath them. The harsh drumming of a fire-frog made him look toward the darkness of the trees. For a fleeting moment he saw the glow of a pair of amber eyes.

He found so many unknown things here. Life on the island was harsh, but much safer. When he reached for his war-hammer, he discovered it gone. He must have left it back by the pond. He wished he had it with him.

They entered the dark opening that led into the temple. The girl walked softly on bare feet. She pulled him deeper into the interior. He had not been aware of it before, but now he detected a musky odor inside the chamber, the smell of decay, of age. They walked through the chamber, past the stone chair, down a narrow, dark corridor.

A few times he scraped his shoulders on cold, slimy stone, but the girl seemed to know their destination. She led him surefooted through the darkness, up some steps, into another chamber.

The dark water of a pond in the center of a huge chamber threw back the reflection of the two moons, visible through an opening in the top. A huge plant floated in the water. Viran saw the silhouette of a woman on the plant.

"The Mother is waiting for you," the girl said. She stepped up to him, kissed him on the lips, turned and disappeared in the darkness.

"Come closer," said the woman on the plant. Her voice sounded husky, seductive, and familiar. Viran remembered Horgan's warning. *The water lilies are carnivorous, never climb onto them!*

He tried to resist the call, but he seemed to be drawn into the water, onto the giant plant. He knelt on the soft petals that grew like a thick carpet on the surface of the plant and looked at the naked woman sitting in front of him.

She looked the same--and yet, different.

Her long flaming hair cascaded around her like a veil. She shook it out of her face, looked into his eyes. "You are Viran," she said and smiled. "Don't be afraid. No harm will come to you while you are with me." Her black eyes seemed to glow with a soft light. She opened her arms. "I have chosen you to be the father of a new generation of my children. Maybe this time I will be more successful."

She rose to her feet, stood in her full glory. His eyes drank from her beauty, traveled over her perfect body, saw the symmetrical face, the large sensuous mouth, and the full lips that revealed white even teeth. The light from the moons set her hair on fire. It spilled down to her ankles, like a sparkling cloak, partially covering her firm round breasts. Below her flat belly a triangle of glowing coppery hair covered a swollen mound.

He stared at her long, slim legs, her strong thighs, as she slowly walked toward him. He became acutely aware of his erection and of his uncontrollable desire for this woman.

She laughed. "Not woman," she said inside his head. "I am The XANDRA. No mortal woman can compare. After this night no woman will ever be able to satisfy your desires the same way that I can. I will be part of you forever. That is the price you pay."

She straddled him. One slim arm reached out, pushed him gently onto his back. He looked into her night-black eyes. They seemed to draw his very soul out of his body.

Very slowly and deliberately she lowered herself onto his stiff sex-organ. Her cleft felt warm and moist, and when her sheath slipped over the swollen head of his member it sent tingling spidery fingers through his entire body. She sank lower. He watched as his aching organ slid deep into her.

He cried out with a hoarse voice and reached up to dig his fingers into her soft breasts. His hips lifted off the ground.

Her black shiny eyes never left his face. She laughed and her body began undulating above him. Her soft, liquid sheath pulsated with gentle pressure around his rigid pole. He swam in a sea of pure pleasure, delirious, his consciousness aware of nothing else but the hot, vibrating living organ that sucked up his very essence.

He erupted inside her with the force of a volcano. Without uncoupling she fell backwards, pulled him on top of her. She wrapped her long legs around him, locked them behind his thighs. Screaming and roaring until his throat became raw, he pumped his hips tirelessly between her cradling soft thighs. She offered her breasts for him to suck on. He swallowed the sweet nectar that flowed from the long thick nipples. Strength flooded through his veins.

Time stood still. He climaxed again. It lasted an eternity.

Chapter Three

When Viran regained his senses, he was alone. Lying on a bed of crushed petals, he looked up into the sky. The moons had disappeared, even Hope, the third one. Reddish fire streaked across the morning sky, announcing the coming of day.

Viran looked around the chamber. He didn't see anyone.

Sitting up, he rubbed his eyes. Had it happened? The memory of the night seemed blurred, but not the picture of *Her*. He remembered her words, *I will be part of you forever.* And so she would be. He would never be able to forget her.

The pond didn't appear very large. Through an open sky light in the ceiling streamed diffused light, playing hide and seek on the lichen and vines that crawled up the rough stones of the walls.

The plant he sat on spread across a quarter of the pond. Its large and thick leaves curled around the center part of the plant. It felt solid underneath his feet when he walked to its edge. Slipping into the water, he found it warm and brackish. He dove under the surface and saw the thick stems and root system that supported the plant.

After climbing out of the water, he looked back, almost expecting to see the woman who had called herself The Xandra, but she did not appear.

Not much light came through the opening above. Tall pillars threw dark shadows inside the chamber. Viran searched in the gloomy twilight for an exit.

When heard the sound of wings above him, he called out, "Angela?" and watched the slim figure landing a short distance away in front of him. He stepped closer, but she turned and began walking away.

"Wait," he called again. When she didn't stop, he ran after her. She disappeared through an opening in the wall. Following her, he entered a dark corridor and cursed loudly when his naked soles stepped on a sharp object, hidden among the debris strewn all over the floor.

He heard her silvery laugh and bumped into her. Her soft small breasts grazed his chest.

"You must be more careful," she whispered and put her arms around him. She felt warm and soft.

He yielded when she pushed him to the rough stone floor. Lying on his back, he saw her silhouetted against the entrance to the corridor.

She spread her wings slightly and straddled him. Hovering above him, her small hands reached down, found his penis, and began fondling it. He reacted with a loud groan, felt his organ grow.

"Don't play with me," he moaned, "unless you can finish what your touch promises."

She laughed again, slowly sank into his lap. Something soft and wet touched the tip of his penis, he felt it open, and then his penis slid into a tight, incredibly soft sheath. "I thought there was no way. You told me you had no desires," he gasped, pushed up.

"I have great desires," she said above him, her voice sounding tight, almost hollow. She began to undulate her body, snapped her pelvis back and forth with forceful thrusts.

He closed his eyes, concentrated on the pleasure in his groin.

She stretched out on top of him, rested her upper body on his chest, while her lower torso kept on pumping. "Tell me when you are ready to release your seed," she whispered into his ear, her cheek warm against his and her hot lips touching his neck.

Feeling the built-up of pressure, he dug his hands into her small buttocks. "Now," he called out. "Now!"

As he erupted inside her he felt a sharp pain in his neck. He cried out in surprise and shock.

Her strength surprised him, as she held him pinned to the ground, while drinking his blood. When she lifted her head, he could see a soft glow in her eyes. "I need very little," she said. "You will not notice the loss. Let me and I will give you more pleasure then you can imagine."

Her hot lips touched his neck. This time he felt no pain. Her sexual organ tightened around his shaft and began to vibrate gently. His fingers were still digging into her soft buttocks. They quivered under his touch. Exquisite pleasure radiated through his body. He began to feel slightly lightheaded, but he didn't care.

After filling her for the third time, she released him. "My desire has been stilled," she whispered. He felt her get up. "You are not Angela," he said, still lying on the ground. He became suddenly aware of a dull pain in his back where the rough surface of the rocks dug into his body.

She laughed, spread her wings. "I never said I was."

"Who are you?"

"I am one of her sisters."

"But you are not like her."

"No, I am her opposite. I am a Shadow Angel, call me Naomi."

He saw her black shadow crouching above him. She took his hand. "Come, I will lead you out of here." He let her pull him up, fought a momentary dizziness when he stood.

"How much of my blood did you drink?"

She chuckled. "Very little. It is a fair bargain. I gave you more than I received."

"How about the seeds I left inside you?" he asked.

"An empty gift." She laughed. "It is of no use to me. Only the nymphs by the pond collect it."

He walked beside her in the darkness. When they turned a corner, he saw light ahead, and then they stepped into another chamber. He recognized it as the one with the stone chair.

"I must leave," Naomi said. In the bright light Viran saw the difference. Her skin was black, almost shiny; her small breasts conical, with a slight up-tilt, not round, like Angela's.

She smiled, displaying two long fangs. "Do you find me attractive and desirable?" she asked.

"I do," Viran answered.

Her dark eyes seemed to mock him. Curling her full, sensuous lips into a smile, she said, "Humans usually find me distasteful. Most would kill me, given the chance. They think I'm evil. How about you? Would you kill me?"

He shook his head. "No, not anymore. I was warned against creatures like you, but I don't think that you are evil."

She looked at him thoughtfully. "All my instincts tell me to avoid Humans. I only seek them out when they are sleeping. But you seem different."

"Why did you seek me?"

Naomie laughed. "My sister--Angela. You seem to have put a spell on her. She has asked the Mother to give her this." She pointed to her genitals. "I don't know why, because she does not feel the way I do. She has no need for it."

Viran knew so little about the creatures of the Xandra, but he knew that they did not propagate like Humans. "Did you find pleasure when you joined with me?" he asked.

She searched his face. "Explain."

He didn't know exactly how. "When I enter you, I feel pleasure. When I give you my seed, I feel greater pleasure through my whole body. Great ecstasy."

She shook her head. "When you enter me, I feel only a piece of your flesh inside me, the same way I feel when I touch you with my hand, but it creates a great hunger in me. When you release your seeds into my body and when I drink your blood at the same time, then I am in ecstasy."

"I think I understand," he nodded. "We are really very different. When I copulate with a female it is for pleasure and propagation. When you copulate with a male it is for feeding." He stared into empty air for a moment. "What a wondrous thing," he mused. "I have much to tell when I get back to my people."

The whispering sound of a pair of large wings made him look up. The golden light from one of the high windows illuminated a white figure gliding toward them.

"My sister," Naomi said.

She came down gently, folded her wings when her feet touched the ground.

"Angela." Viran smiled. "This time it is you."

Angela's blue eyes looked at Naomi. "Did you give him what he craved?" she asked.

The dark girl laughed. "He craves you, sister. I cannot give him that, and neither can you. I took what I needed." She spread her great black wings and took to the air.

Viran watched her land on the edge of one of the windows. She climbed through, then she disappeared. He looked at Angela. "I thought it was you," he explained. "I wish it had been you."

She put her hand to her crotch, cupped it. "It is like Naomi said, I have nothing to give you, and you have nothing that I need." Her eyes looked at him sadly.

He walked up to her and put his hand under chin. "You are so lovely," he said, took her face between his hands and kissed her. Her slim arms went around his neck. She pressed her body against his, her small breasts warm and soft against his chest. As his penis stiffened, he slid it between her soft thighs.

She broke the kiss, pushed him away. "It is useless," she said, "my skin tingles strangely when you touch me, but that is all."

"You could take it into your mouth," he suggested.

"What would that do for me?"

He shrugged. "I don't know, probably nothing, but it's worth a try."

She fell to her knees in front of him and took his rigid mast into her small hands. Then she touched it with her tongue, parted her lips and sucked him slowly into her mouth. He moaned, put his hands around her head and pumped his pelvis back and forth. When he erupted he held her tight. He felt her struggle, but he didn't release her until he finished.

She pulled back her head, her cheeks puffed up. She swallowed, and then she spit onto the ground. "It has a strange taste," she said, licking her lips. "Maybe it is good nourishment."

"Did you enjoy it?" he asked.

She shook her head. "No, did you?"

"Yes, I did, but a mouth does not replace the flower. I wish you were like your sister."

Her blue eyes seemed sad. "I am not my sister. I am me. It saddens me that you prefer her to me."

"No, no." He pulled her to him. "I prefer you. It is just…"

She slipped out of his embrace. "We cannot change what is. Only the Mother can. I have asked her to change me." She turned and walked out of the chamber. "Come, I will guide you to the pond."

He followed her slowly. Watching the tips of her feathery wings trail on the ground, he admired the play of her small round buttocks as she walked in front of him.

Why did he feel so attracted to her? She was not even human. She could never give him what he needed as a man. Only a fool would fall for someone like her.

The path ended. When he stepped into the clearing he found it deserted. His breeches, boots, and war-hammer lay at the edge of the pond. "Where is everybody?" he asked the winged girl.

Angela shrugged her delicate shoulders. "The water nymphs have gone back to their nests; your friends left early this morning."

"Without me?"

"It appears so." Angela spread her wings and lifted into the air. "I must leave you now." She blew him a kiss and beating her wings furiously she soared upwards.

After watching her slim lovely form disappear beyond the treetops, he went to retrieve his possession. When his sore feet slipped into the soft-soled boots his spirits went up. He bent to pick up his war-hammer, raised it high into the air in a silent salute. Alone he might be, but his courage and strength would be his companions and the Great Spirit of Thunder would guide him home.

Walking back the narrow trail, he found himself at the steps of the old temple. It didn't look as foreboding in the light of day. Now he only saw decaying crumbling stonewalls, which the surrounding forest vegetation tried to reclaim.

Searching the soft ground for tracks, he found footprints leading toward one of the many trails that led to the temple. Shouldering his big hammer, he proceeded to follow the tracks.

He wondered why they left him behind. Again he questioned Horgan's abilities to lead the gathering-team. It was the leader's responsibility to bring back every member of the team, even a dead one, if at all possible. Obviously, they didn't make much of an effort to find him.

The path twisted and turned through the forest, many times branching into different directions. Viran had not been paying attention to the tracks, assuming his companions were following the wider path. His eyes were watching the trees, fearing attacks from above.

Not only the night harbored deadly creatures.

He realized suddenly that there were no more human footprints on the path. Also, it grew darker. He should have caught up with his friends by now. Turning around, he followed his own footsteps back, but soon it became too dark to make them out clearly. When he looked up, he noticed the dark clouds in the overcast sky. It looked like rain, and the moons would not be visible this night.

Time to look for shelter.

He found it at the base of a giant Kopka-tree. Crawling under the gnarled entwined roots, he made himself as comfortable as possible. The thick branches above him kept most of the rain away from him and soon the rustling of the leaves told him that the first drops were beginning to fall.

He wished for his warm cloak, but because of the weather at this time of year he left it behind. Besides, it would have been cumbersome to carry.

It didn't take long before the water pooled on the path and small rivulets began to run into his hiding place. Feeling miserable and shivering from the chill, he drew his aching body into a ball and tried to catch some sleep.

Chapter Four

"There are no signs of life from any of the towers? Are you certain?" Commander Beringer stared into the large purple eyes of Starfinder.

The alien shrugged. The similarities between the two species constantly amazed Beringer

"One thousand years is a long time, much can happen," Starfinder said. "Maybe they abandoned the station and moved down to the planet."

Beringer looked at the unfamiliar instruments and at the empty screens, which they didn't dare to power up for fear that some unseen enemy might detect them. He shook his head. "There were the shuttles and the battle cruiser. I just can't imagine that they would give up the station, especially with all of us still alive. Maybe they didn't perceive us as a threat."

"I think we should send out a team and check it out," Starfinder said.

"Do you think it's wise?" Beringer asked. He still didn't trust the silence, which the scanners reported. What if it was a trap to flush them out? What if Captain Cunningham...? He stopped himself. Captain Cunningham died a long time ago. Over a thousand years passed since the Xandra invaded the station and changed every human into something alien. Everyone, except Commander Beringer and his marines. Thanks to Starfinder, who lived through a similar nightmare a thousand years earlier, they discovered the awful truth and took refuge deep in the bowels of the giant space station. They slept in cryogenic suspension for a thousand years, waiting for rescue.

Starfinder programmed a small number of modules to awaken their sleepers after a certain time had elapsed.

Commander Beringer and half a dozen of his men were among the ones chosen. Ten of the aliens had also been revived. Five males and five females.

They had been awake now for two weeks.

"I'll take two of my men and a couple of yours," Beringer said. "I need to know what is going on."

"I agree," said the alien leader, "I will come with you."

"Don't you think you should stay behind?"

Starfinder smiled. "I am not indispensable. I also must know."

Beringer shrugged, but said nothing. He kept staring at the giant blank screen on the wall, useless without power, but they wouldn't turn on the power for the whole station until they knew what had happened.

Not for the first time Beringer marveled over the Space Station. It's size alone testified to the highly advanced technology of the aliens. They called themselves Genaar, which meant *Above Animals*. They were not a warlike race, unlike the Humans, whose history is riddled with constant wars and great bloodshed. So far Humans had not encountered another species that possessed technology and great intelligence, except for one planet in the Alpha Centauri system with humanoids barely above the stage of the apes on Earth. They did live in a loose tribal society, had rudimentary tools and used weapons for hunting, but that did not qualify them as an intelligent species. Especially since massive quantities of various metal deposits had been discovered on that planet.

Beringer did not know which part of the Galaxy the Genaar came from. Starfinder had not elaborated. He usually acted somewhat evasive when asked. The Commander had the distinct impression that Starfinder did not quite trust the Humans.

When the Humans originally discovered the sleeping Genaar (a thousand years ago!), they only saw the chamber that housed the cryogenic modules.

The core of the sphere held the power generators, the heart of the space station. No organic life form was allowed to enter there. The radiation would kill anyone foolish enough to do so. Actually, nobody could access the core. It was sealed off completely from the rest of the station. Mobile computers watched and maintained it, serviced it when necessary.

Commander Beringer never did have a chance to see much of even the floor they where on, or the ones above, but what he saw impressed him greatly.

There were living quarters for the crew, exercise rooms, and cooking facilities. Starfinder confided in the Commander and told him that they had enough food in storage to keep everyone alive for a hundred years, everything kept in cryogenic suspension, just like the sleepers. Beringer wondered what else hid in the bowels of the sphere.

"I want Starmote to be on the team," Starfinder broke into Beringer's thoughts. "She has been on missions before. Also, she is the closest to what classifies as a soldier."

The commander looked sharply at the alien. "I thought you people did not practice warfare?"

Starfinder smiled. "We don't, but others do."

Beringer left it at that. He studied the alien with mixed feelings, suspecting much more hidden underneath Starfinder's gentle manner. It wouldn't do to underestimate him. He sighed and relaxed. He had nothing to fear from these people. They were his allies, his friends. And yet--he was a soldier, trained to be suspicious.

Trust no one, not even a friend!

"Whatever you say," he said aloud. "I don't expect to walk into a hostile situation. It's been a thousand years, and it looks like everyone is dead anyway."

"On the station, but we don't know what to expect on the planet." Starfinder glanced at the big screen. "Once we have power throughout the station we can send a probe down to the surface."

"I'd like to go down there myself."

Starfinder shook his head. "Not advisable, until we know what we are dealing with." He smiled. "You are an impatient man, Commander. In my long life I have learned to be more cautious. It helped me live this long."

"I am a soldier, my friend. I am trained to be cautious, but sometimes you have to take the initiative. Attack instead of waiting."

"We never attack anyone," Starfinder said thoughtfully, "and our species ranges far. If my people and yours ever face each other, I hope there will be no reason for an attack. It is not always the attacker who wins."

A disguised threat? A subtle warning? Beringer wasn't certain. One thing he became sure of more and more, the Genaar were not as peaceful as they seemed. A race of people who spread themselves across many star systems cannot afford to be. It would be wise to be their friend.

"Have you ever encountered hostile races?" he asked.

"Many."

"What happened?"

Starfinder shrugged. "We convinced them that it wouldn't be a good idea to be our enemy."

"I'll remember that," Beringer said.

"We are friends." Starfinder smiled, a twinkle in his dark eyes. "I don't believe that you will need convincing."

One of the alien females came into the room. Beringer remembered the first time he and the other human men saw the alien females. They were smitten by their beauty. All the females he had seen so far were somewhat petite, with delicate features.

This one looked different, taller, more muscular, but just as beautiful. Her movements, though graceful and fluid, reminded Beringer of the great cats that roamed the protected jungles on Earth.

She nodded toward Beringer when she walked in, her large eyes dark and smoldering. Shaking her thick black hair out of her face, she gave him a little smile. Then she turned toward Starfinder and said something in the language of the aliens.

Beringer did not understand her and made a mental note to ask for a translation device.

"You will be on the team," he heard Starfinder say to the female. Only Starfinder possessed a translator.

Another one of the amazing devices of the aliens

"Tell her that I am the leader, and tell her also that she will have to take orders from me," he told the alien.

Starfinder nodded. "No need to tell her," he said "She knows. And don't worry, she is the best."

"I hope we don't have to find out," the Commander murmured to himself. Aloud he said, "I want to leave tomorrow, but now I'd like to check out our weapon's status and the state of the power generators. I hope they're still operating. I also want to make sure that our space suits are still working." He paused, then, with a glance at the girl, "I cannot communicate with her without a translator. Can you fit me with one?"

"That was my next suggestion," Starfinder said and smiled again. "I think we will work well together, you and I. Our thoughts seem to overlap sometimes. That is good."

* * * *

They called her Starmote.

Again, Beringer wondered how much else the aliens were hiding. Starmote had not been among the females the Humans revived after discovering the Genaar. That left one obvious conclusion. There were more cryogenic chambers, on this deck or on one of the decks closer to the core. Maybe they hid a whole army hidden somewhere.

He put it out of his mind and followed the woman down a corridor. She walked slightly ahead of him, moved silently on soft-soled boots. Her tight body suit left nothing to the imagination, and he caught himself watching the soft play of her round buttocks. *Damn*! he thought, *this alien female is turning me on. She's supposed to be a soldier. Soldiers don't dress this way.* His thoughts drifted to Breanna, the last woman he made love to. He chuckled. A thousand years ago. *Wonder, what happened to her.*

They entered a lab where two of the males were busy testing equipment. Starmote spoke to them. One of them walked to a cabinet, opened it and removed a small metal box, and then he motioned for Beringer to sit in a chair. He moved behind the Commander. Beringer heard the clinking of metal instruments. The alien said something, but Beringer didn't, of course, understand a word. The touch of cold metal behind his ear and the gentle pressure as the alien pushed a tiny object under his skin sent minute shocks into his brain. After a moment of disorientation he felt nothing at all.

"You should understand me now," said the alien. "But you won't be able to talk until I insert the modem into your throat."

Again, Beringer felt no pain, just some discomfort, as the technician pressed the small device against Beringer's larynx.

The alien walked away, sat down at his desk. When Beringer didn't move he looked up and smiled. "You're all done. You can talk now, if you want to."

Beringer cleared his throat. "I hope this works," he said. "I can understand you, but can you understand me?"

"I can."

"This is amazing. How does it work?"

The alien technician shrugged. "I don't really know. I am not a scientist."

When he walked back with Starmote he remarked, "You look different from the other women I've seen."

She looked at him from the side. "I am different. Do I look ugly to you?"

"Oh, not all." He lifted his hands. "You are very beautiful, but the others, they're more, well, demure, softer in their manners."

"I was not designed to be soft," she said.

"Designed?"

"My designation was decided before I was born. I have no desire to be anything else. Nothing about me is random. I am a perfect specimen."

"With a heavy dose of deceit," Beringer mumbled. "I wonder how you are in bed."

She stopped, put a hand on his chest. "I have perfect hearing, Beringer. Besides, those translators have one drawback, they translate everything into clear audible language. If you want to know how I am, as you put it, in bed, let's go to my quarters and you can find out." Her large dark eyes flashed with suppressed anger and between her full lips gleamed white teeth.

Something about her turned him on, and he felt a sudden desire to take her up on her invitation. He pulled her to him, kissed her fiercely. She responded almost as fiercely. Her hand went down to his crotch, found his hardness.

She pulled away, suddenly, laughed. "Maybe I'll let you find out, but not today."

He wiped his mouth, stared at her. "Don't be a bitch!" he said angrily. When she turned and walked away, he grabbed her shoulder, spun her around. Still smiling, she fell into a crouch, whirled and smashed her foot into his chest. He fell backwards, sprawled onto the floor.

She stood over him, glared. "I am not like the others, I do attack."

He rubbed his chest, looked up at her. "Another surprise. What else has Starfinder up his sleeve?"

She offered her hand, pulled him up. "I am not your enemy. This was just a small demonstration. I want you to think of me as a full member of your team." She smiled, looking sweet and innocent, brushed her lips against his. "About the other thing, we'll see."

Chapter Five

It had stopped raining. Viran tried to lie as quietly as possible, no easy task in his cramped quarters. The gnarled roots of the Kapka-tree had eventually given up the fight against the assaulting water from above. They felt cold and slimy against his bare skin.

He didn't sleep much, but he must have dozed off. The squish-squish of bare feet on the muddy trail brought him to instant alertness. They stopped close to his hiding place. He couldn't see anything in the complete darkness, but the stench of rotting flesh overpowered the musky, wet odor of the decaying leaves he lay on.

Zombs.

He stilled his breathing, but it proved useless. They could see him in the dark and they could smell *fresh meat* from faraway.

A cold, clammy hand touched his shoulder. Strong bony fingers dug into his arms and pulled him out of his uncomfortable resting place. He tried to use his war-hammer, but they ripped it out of his grip. How many there were he had no idea. They moved silently without even an occasional grunt. After tying his hands behind his back and his legs at the ankles, they pulled him through the wet mud like the dead carcass of a food-animal.

They dragged him over fallen trees and rocks, leaving his body with painful bruises. Luckily, the wet ground saved him from greater punishment.

Suddenly, the trail became rough and hard. Viran winced when sharp pebbles cut his skin. He still couldn't see anything. It seemed even darker now than before.

He noticed a definite decline and knew that they had entered some underground caverns.

Trapped in the lair of the Zombs!

They left him lying, bound and helpless.

He took a few deep breaths and gagged from the stench that assaulted his nostrils. Trying to relax, he became aware of every muscle and bone in his body.

Listening, he heard the drip-drip of water, but then he detected the soft sound of breathing.

"Is anyone here?" he asked.

Still silence, but now heard the gentle rustling of someone moving.

"I am Viran," he said. "Who are you?"

"Are you human?" asked a female voice.

Viran turned his head in the direction the voice had come from. "I was once," he said, chuckling, and coughed when pain from bruised ribs shot through his body. "Now I'm not so sure."

"What you mean?"

"I mean that I am nothing but tenderized meat for the Zombs." He coughed again and tried to move into a more comfortable position.

"Zombs. Is that what these creatures are called?"

"You didn't know? Where do you come from?"

"We are lost travelers," another female voice said. Even though her voice seemed strained it still sounded soft and pleasant. She spoke with a peculiar accent, just like her companion.

"How many of you are there?" Viran asked.

"Just the two of us," said the first voice. "I am Mirtin and my companion is Vienne."

"What are these… these Zombs going to do with us?" asked Vienne.

Viran started laughing, but stopped and groaned. "We've been invited for dinner, and you and I are the main course."

"Cannibals!" Vienne cursed. "We've been captured by a bunch of cannibals."

"Viran," the woman, who had identified herself as Mirtin, said, "you seem to be in pain. Are you injured?"

"Not seriously, I think, but my whole body is aching."

"I can help you." The woman hesitated a little. "If you are human, I can give you something for the pain."

Viran heard the scraping sounds as she crept toward him. "Let me look at you," the voice said softly beside his year. Viran closed his eyes when a sudden brightness flared up in front of his face.

"Sorry," the woman said, "I didn't mean to startle you like that. You can open your eyes now."

When he did, he looked into a pair of gray eyes, human eyes. A dim light, which she cupped with one hand, illuminated the woman's face, highlighting her high cheekbones and slightly slanted eyes. She seemed young, but somehow Viran had the impression that she was much older than she appeared to be.

He couldn't tell what her body looked like underneath the loose fitting outfit she wore.

"I guess you'll pass for human," she said and wrinkled her nose. "What did you do? Roll in the mud?"

Viran chuckled. "Something like that. It'll wash off. What about my pain?"

"Oh, right." She took something out of a pouch that hung from a belt she wore around her waist and began rubbing a spot on his upper arm. "My, you've got some biceps," she murmured and let her hand travel across his chest. Her hand felt smooth and warm.

"For heaven's sakes, Mirtin," said her companion, "stop admiring his physique. He's a savage."

"He's a man," Mirtin said.

"So he is." Vienne sighed audibly. "Give him the painkiller and maybe he can get us out of here."

Mirtin pressed something against the spot she had cleaned. It stung for a moment. Viran felt a gentle tingling sensation in his arm.

"Give it a minute to enter your blood stream," Mirtin said, studying Viran. Her eyes widened suddenly.

"You are bound. No wonder you look so uncomfortable." She pulled an object out of her boot. It reflected the light that came from her other hand.

A long, thin-bladed knife. Viran had never seen one like it. His feet and arms were tied together with tough vines, but the keen-edged blade cut through them without sawing motions.

"You possess wondrous things," he said as he rubbed his wrists to return circulation to his hands. "The cold fire in your hand that burns without heat, the knife, the medicine. You must come from a place very far from here."

"Very far indeed." The other woman, Vienne, had seated herself cross-legged in front of Viran and stared at him out of deep blue eyes. She looked younger than Mirtin, her face more delicate than that of her companion. With her blond, almost white hair, she reminded Viran of Angela, the winged girl. He noticed that both women had their hair cropped close to their skull. In some strange way he did find it attractive.

Judging from their light skin, neither of the women spent much time outside under the sun. Viran's own skin, especially on his upper body, had taken on a deep bronze shade. In the warm season he usually wore just breeches. Only on cold nights, or when the days became shorter and cooler, did he wear a cloak.

"How did you get captured by the Zombs?" he asked.

"We were looking for shelter from the rain. These caves looked good, but we soon found out that they were occupied." Vienne made a face. "I guess the stench should have given us a clue."

"What are these creatures?" Mirtin asked. "We've only got glimpses of them in the dark."

"They are the Zombs," Viran shrugged, "I don't know much about them. They're not very smart. They shun the light, it hurts their eyes, but they can see at night."

"And they stink like rotting flesh. You said they eat people?"

"People, Tree-devils, even Neanders, anything that is meat." He grinned. "The first thing they'll eat will be your breasts, because they like soft and tender morsels."

Vienne crossed her arms over her breasts in a defensive gesture. "You're kidding, I hope."

"No, I'm not, and the bigger they are, the better."

"Well, then Vienne won't have to worry too much," chuckled Mirtin.

"Oh, shut up!" Vienne's blue eyes flashed. "Not everybody has tits like you."

"Don't give away secrets now, Blue-Eyes." Mirtin looked at Viran. "Are you well enough to travel?" she asked. "You don't look too good."

Viran stood, stretched and grimaced when his sore muscles protested. "I've felt better, but also worse. Can you help me find my war-hammer with that light of yours? I'm sure they left it in here."

"Your war-hammer? Oh, a weapon."

Mirtin swept the cave they where in, in her hand the light had become brighter. Vienne gave a little shriek when it illuminated a pile of white bones. Caved-in skulls told of the brutal way their owners had died.

"This is horrible," she said. "In what kind of savage place did they set us down?"

"Keep your thoughts to yourself!" Mirtin warned her sharply. Putting a hand on the younger girl's arm, she said softly, "Sorry, the first assignments are usually the toughest. But unfortunately it doesn't get any better, you just get used to it."

"If we survive this." Vienne said sourly

"We will, Blue-Eyes, we will. I have great confidence in our new-found local hero." Mirtin let the light linger on Viran. "Look at him! Look at those muscles, nothing can stop him. I've never seen such a healthy savage looking specimen of a man."

"Can't you wait until we're in a safe place before you try to seduce him," Vienne said sullenly. "My opinion of him isn't that great; after all, he didn't come here of his own free will, bound the way he was. He's an uncivilized barbarian."

"Do all women in your tribe discuss males so freely in front of them?" Viran asked. "I can't make much sense of some of the things you're saying, but I'm not an ignorant Neander." He looked at Vienne. "If we were *in a safe place* you'd be spreading your legs for me by now."

"What? You crazy, conceded…" Vienne exploded and sprang to her feet.

Mirtin laughed. "Take it easy, Blue-Eyes. He doesn't know about you."

"That's right. I've never spread my legs for any man and I never will, and neither should you. He's filthy."

"Can we keep looking for my hammer?" Viran asked, raising his voice.

They found it lying by the entrance. Viran went to pick it up, hefted it in his hands. It felt good to touch the worn handle and feel the weight of the iron head. "I'm ready," he said.

"Magnificent!" Mirtin breathed and sighed audibly. "I hope we make it out alive."

"Oh, Mirtin, you are so hopeless." Vienne lifted her hands and rolled her eyes, then she followed Viran and Mirtin. They stepped into a narrow corridor. Mirtin let her light play over the slimy, wet rocky walls.

"Which way?" Viran asked.

Vienne glared at him. "You don't know?"

"I was not exactly in a position to orient myself," Viran countered.

"Oh, that's right, I forgot. You were tied up," Vienne sneered.

It was Viran's turn to glare. "Listen, girl, you better hold your tongue, before I…"

"Before you what?" Vienne stood in front of him, hands on her hips.

Viran's hand shot out suddenly. He grabbed her by the neck and pulled her close, crushed his lips against hers. The girl struggled and beat her fists against his strong arms. Bringing up her knee, she kicked him in the groin.

He let go of her and stepped back, grinning. "You'll have to kick me harder if you want to hurt me, Blue-Eyes."

Vienne wiped her mouth and spat. "Wait until the painkillers wear off, you'll know where I hurt you!"

"Stop it, you two!" Mirtin said sharply. She stared at Vienne. "What's gotten into you? He's our ally, not our enemy. He may be our only chance to get back, so don't mess it up! That's an order!"

"Yes, sir." Vienne straightened out, her eyes blanked over momentarily. "I'm sorry. It won't happen again."

"It better not. Now let's get out of here." Mirtin's voice had a cold edge to it. She didn't sound at all like the gentle woman she seemed to be when she tended Viran. These women were not like the women Viran was used to.

Females in his tribe did not carry knives in their boots or anywhere else on their bodies. Knives were used for cutting vegetables and meat.

The code only allowed a warrior to possess weapons. Women did the cooking, cleaning, household chores, and raise the children. They took care of the food animals and tended the gardens.

And they spread their legs for a man, willingly, without making a big fuss.

Viran shook his head. *I wonder what the men are like where these two come from.*

He sniffed the air. Above the stench of rotting flesh and feces that filled his nostrils he detected the scent of fresh air. He began to walk in the direction of the barely noticeable air current. Mirtin walked beside him, her light illuminating the crooked corridors ahead of them.

Viran stopped suddenly, held up his hand. His keen hearing had detected a shuffling sound.

"Around the corner," he whispered and grabbed his war-hammer with both hands.

"How do you know?" asked Vienne behind him.

"I can smell them." Viran bared his teeth, grinned viciously. "Now you can show me what you're made of Blue-Eyes. There is no easy way out of here."

He glanced at Mirtin. "Use your light," he said. "Bright light hurts their eyes and makes them blind. Let's rush them."

Bunching his muscles, he sprang around the corner, Mirtin right behind him. His big hammer smashed into a skull. It exploded with a dull sound, spraying purple ichor. The creature crumpled to the ground. He brought down his weapon on another bald head. The cracking of bone sounded like the snapping of a dry tree branch.

There were three more of the Zombs, but they just stood there, their large hands thrown across their faces, to protect their eyes from the glare of the bright light in Mirtin's hand.

Something crackled beside Viran. A bolt of lightning hit one of the three remaining creatures. Viran stared for a short moment at the huge hole that had appeared in the Zomb's chest. The acrid smell of burnt meat rose up in his nostrils. He looked at Vienne, who stood beside Mirtin, saw her move her hand slightly, then another bright bolt left her hand, and then another. He heard the sound of three falling bodies.

Vienne glanced at Viran, her face seemed without emotion, and her eyes gleamed like blue ice. "Did I prove myself?" she said to him, almost with a snarl.

He nodded slowly, his right hand tightening around the handle of his war-hammer. It would not do to underestimate these two women, especially Vienne. He would have to tread very carefully around them. He looked at the corpses on the ground and shuddered slightly. Their bodies were covered with huge boils and open sores. Patches of coarse hair grew from rotting skin. Once they had been human. Not true Humans, for they were creations of the Xandra, but human-like. True Humans, if they lived long enough, died of old age, not so the Xandra-Humans. They became Zombs.

Viran didn't understand the whole process, but his teacher, Orin the Historian, taught him this when he was young.

Wise, old Orin, he knew many things. Some of them hard to believe and understand. He knew much about the Xandra and her creatures, and why Viran's people lived on the harsh island. Viran had never really cared much, he liked the island. It was safe. But if he ever got back he just might ask Old Orin to teach him more of his secret knowledge.

"Let's move on," Mirtin said beside him. "Lead the way."

Viran sniffed the air again, took the tunnel to his right.

They had only taken a few steps when another group of Zombs confronted them, a large group, too many for Viran to fight, possibly too many even for Vienne's lightning bolts.

Chapter Six

The six space-suited figures moved cautiously down the high-ceilinged corridor. Even with the main power of the station off, the gravity generators were working, making traveling somewhat difficult. Space suits were not designed for walking.

Commander Beringer felt sorry now that he insisted he and his men wore Earth-designed suits. The alien space suits, like most of the devices the Genaar possessed, were obviously of superior design, more form-fitting and lighter, they allowed for easier, quicker movements.

Even though they had come this way before (a thousand years ago!), everything looked unfamiliar. When they fled into the cryogenic chamber the station had still been alive, with lights illuminating every corner. Now it was dark, cold. Their headlamps threw long, eerie shadows, and Beringer saw movement behind every column or piece of machinery. *Just my imagination*, he told himself, but his nerves were raw, on edge, the terror of the Xandra's silent invasion still fresh in his mind.

Thousand years may have passed, but for him only barely three weeks, since he watched the Captain and most of the crew members turn into parodies of human beings.

Who knew what lurked in the shadows, waiting to pounce on them.

"The stairs should be ahead." Starmote's voice came through the speaker behind his ear. She had studied the layout of the levels above them and mapped the route.

It would have been easier to move between decks had the elevators been working. But with the power down they had to do it the hard way. Most of the decks had ceilings about 25 meters high, but then there were still five meters of crawlspace, which meant 30 meters of stairs for one floor. They had four decks to climb until they came to the outermost level, with a ceiling 100 meters high.

Thick, airtight doors, which could be operated manually, sealed off every deck from the next.

They passed the useless elevators. Beringer gave them a disappointed look.

When the small group arrived in front of the door that led into the staircase, Starmote cautioned everyone to stand clear. Very slowly she turned the wheel that opened the door. Pulling the heavy door open, she stepped through. "All clear," she said from the other side.

Beringer relaxed, followed her into the dark interior. Looking up, he saw a black hole above him. The part of the staircase his and Starmote's head lamp illuminated seemed to disappear into a dark void.

"Starfinder," Beringer said into his mike, "are you sure you want to accompany us all the way? It will be a long and strenuous climb."

The alien laughed softly and touched Beringer's arm. "Don't insult me, Commander. I may be old, but I am not feeble."

Beringer had not realized that the alien leader stood beside him. Turning his head inside his transparent helmet, he chuckled. "I didn't mean any disrespect, I am just concerned."

"I appreciate that. But let us not waste any time, start climbing."

Having been frozen for a thousand years had left no ill effects on Beringer. He felt fit and fully capable of enduring hardships, and yet, when they finally reached the top he almost needed a rest.

These damn suits, he cursed silently, *I wish I would not have been so stubborn and taken Starfinder's advice. He's not even breathing hard.*

"Only five hundred more steps to climb, Commander." The alien's voice sounded cheerful in his ears. "How are you holding up, my alien friend?"

Beringer sighed. It sounded strange to hear Starfinder talk like that, but to the Genaar the Humans were the aliens. "I'm alright," he said, "just not used to climbing stairs."

Starmote busied herself with the next set of doors and managed to get them to open. They stepped into a bare room, up a flight of stairs and stood facing the door to the next deck. Starmote entered the darkened staircase. The others followed slowly. They could gain entry into the deck through a door on the other side.

"Shall we check out this level?" Beringer asked Starfinder.

"No, there is nothing there," the alien answered, "I'd like to get up to the outer level as fast as possible. I need to know what happened."

Beringer found himself counting steps as he climbed behind Starmote, but gave it up soon. Behind him came Starfinder, then Moonwanderer, the scientist in Starfinder's team. Lt. Wang and space-marine Lambert made up the rear.

Both carried laser-rifles.

Beringer's hand went down to his hip, touched his own weapon. He was hoping that there would be no need to ever use it.

When Starmote finally opened the last door, Lt. Wang and Lambert stood ready with their weapons, but nothing threatening waited on the other side.

They stepped into the docking bay. From above, through a large transparent oval opening in the ceiling, starlight fell onto the small battle-cruiser that had been part of the colonist's armament.

Beringer stared at it, almost with resentment. So much power, just sitting there, and it had been useless against the enemy, the *Xandra*.

They began walking in the direction of the tower that had been occupied by the Humans. Looking up at the ceiling that lay a hundred meters above them, Beringer wondered how they would get up there. They had no means to reach it, there were no stairs. It might as well be a thousand meters, it didn't matter. The elevators, which could have transported them up into the tower, did not work.

"What now?" he asked.

"There are many things you do not know about this station, Commander." Starfinder said.

"Like what?"

"You'll see. Starmote knows what to do."

Beringer watched Starmote walk away. Even though her space suite didn't exactly fit like a second skin, it was quite obvious that a female, occupied it, a female with generous curves. He felt a sudden gentle stirring in his loins and realized again that he had been without female companionship for a long time. He didn't know what attracted him to her, she was not soft and cuddly, like the others, she had quite clearly demonstrated her aggressiveness. She was dangerous, unpredictable, but maybe that was it. Beringer was a soldier, trained to enter dangerous territory.

"She was not bred to please a man." Starfinder's voice came softly over the speaker. "She is a soldier, like you."

Beringer gave the alien leader a startled look. His head lamp fell on Starfinder's face, displayed a smile.

"You are very perceptive," Beringer said, "or are you reading my mind?"

Starfinder chuckled. "I saw it in your eyes when you first met her."

The commander didn't say any more. No need for his men to know how he felt toward Starmote. Since they didn't have any translators they could only understand what he said.

"Here she comes," Starfinder said.

A small vehicle came silently toward them. It stopped in front of the group. Beringer entered it first. Glancing at Starmote, who sat at the controls, he noticed a couple of bench seats on either side of the interior.

"Sit down, Commander," Starmote said and chuckled, "we will ride in comfort."

"You people never fail to amaze me," he said as Starfinder joined him. "Can you use this vehicle in space?"

"No, it is too slow. It was designed to transport people inside the cargo bay."

Starmote took the small vehicle up, landed it on a platform just below the ceiling. They got out, walked toward a closed door. Beringer saw another, larger cargo door, further down, but they needed power to open that one.

"Looks like this door can only be opened from the other side," Starmote said. "We'll have to slice through the lock."

"What if there is air on the other side?" Beringer protested. "It'll blow us off this platform."

"Stand aside then. I'll drill a very small hole first, but I don't believe there is any danger. We won't find any air."

The bright blue thin pencil of light burnt a hole through the door in a very short time.

Nothing happened.

Starmote proceeded to cut a circle large enough for them to climb through. Beringer surveyed the small room, looked at the door on the other side. "What about that one?" he asked.

"That one I can open." Starmote studied a small screen beside the door. "It is dead," she announced, "there is nothing on the other side but empty vacuum." She opened the door, stepped through. Lt. Wang and space-marine Lambert were close behind her with drawn weapons.

"It is safe, Commander," came the report from Lt. Wang.

Beringer and the rest of the team followed.

They stood in another staircase that led up to the first floor. Again, Starmote began climbing the stairs first. When she opened the door into the corridor of the first floor they still found nothing to indicate that Humans had ever occupied this tower.

The first floor had been used to store the huge water tanks. They found them, cracked open, the floor was covered with large chunks of ice. On the third floor they found the first Humans, or what remained of them. Five naked skeletons covered with lumpy pieces of flesh and gray skin, their faces caricatures of what they once had looked like.

In another room they found a pile of bones with gnaw marks on them. Two skulls, pieces of hair sticking to them, lay not far from the pile. Both skulls were cracked open.

"What happened here, Commander?" Even over the speaker Lambert's voice betrayed the terror he felt inside.

"Looks like they tried to eat each other." Starfinder picked up one of the skulls. "The brain matter has been sucked out of this one."

Silently they moved on, up another flight of stairs. On every floor they found human remains. All were in a state of decay, some were human, and others looked like monstrous obscenities.

They found Captain Cunningham, slumped over his desk, in his quarters on the seventh floor, with his door sealed shut. They had to force their way in. In his frozen, bony fingers he held a small laser pistol. Lumpy sores covered his face and body. A pile of bound books were stacked on his desk, one open, in front of him, partially covered by his rigid body.

His personal logbooks, every entry in his neat handwriting.

Beringer felt a lump form in his throat. In the few months he spent under the captain's command, they became good friends.

Captain Cunningham had been a hopeless romantic. Why else would a man insist in keeping a handwritten journal? What an archaic way to keep a record when it would have been so much easier and faster to enter it into the electronic data-bank.

"Lambert," Beringer said, "take care of these logbooks. I have a feeling they'll provide us with some answers."

"Yes, Sir, Commander!" Lambert removed his back-pack, proceeded to put the journals into it. Before he packed the last one, he stopped and glanced at the opened page. Shrugging, he closed the book carefully and added it to the others.

"What did you read?" Beringer asked softly.

"Nothing, Sir, nothing."

"Good, keep it to yourself, for now. These are the Captain's personal thoughts. They should be treated with respect."

Beringer walked over to the porthole that showed a portion of space. The huge globe of Nu-Eden hung in front of him, mysterious and silent, half of it illuminated by its Primary. The other half lay in darkness.

He sensed the presence of someone beside him. "He loved this view," he said.

"Beautiful, isn't it?" Starfinder's voice came softly over the speaker. "It looks so peaceful."

"That's why we named it Nu-Eden," Beringer said. "This was supposed to be a paradise."

"We never gave it a name, just a number." Starfinder chuckled. "Even though, one of our poets called it *Song of Despair*. I didn't have to ask him why."

"I don't think we have to climb any higher." Beringer tore himself away from the porthole. We know what we'll find. There is nothing alive in this tower."

"I agree." Starfinder stood for another moment looking out into space, then he, too, turned away from it. "We will seal off this tower out of respect for the dead. I'd like to power up the whole station again, close it off against any intruders."

"Intruders?" asked Beringer.

"Just a precaution. Remember, we've been out of touch for a long time, a thousand years for you, about eight hundred of our years. We don't know what occurred during that time."

"You are right. I wonder what happened to our exploration ship. Did it ever come back, or did it meet up with some disaster? Why didn't anybody ever come from Earth?"

"Maybe they did." Starfinder put a gloved hand on the commander's arm. "Let us study your captain's logbooks. Maybe some of your questions will be answered."

Chapter Seven

Excerpts from Captain Cunningham's Log
AD 2985 to AD 3015

I've been down to Nu-Eden a few times now. The settlers of the second phase are still True-Humans. They have split into three groups. One group decided to join Alpha-Colony, the other two went on their own.

None of the True-Humans know what the Xandra has done to the first phase of settlers.

It might create problems.

But they do know about the Xandra.

* * * *

The small attachment of soldiers we had stationed at Alpha Colony under the command of Sergeant Vicks has moved north into an area where the Xandra cannot exist.

The only way a man can be changed is by direct contact with the giant plant. The Xandra will appear as a beautiful woman, one that appeals to the individual she wants to change. Sexual intercourse takes place. The man's seed is taken and used for fertilization. The body of the man is then absorbed. The Xandra creates a clone and transfers all the memories of the original individual.

The new body doesn't age, it is always healthy.

Sergeant Vicks and his troopers never went through this process.

* * * *

The True-Humans are breeding fiercely. Many babies are born.

The Xandra-Humans are not fertile. The only way the Xandra can reproduce more Humans is through the seed pouches.

And she needs True-Human males to fertilize them.

* * * *

The Xandra is experimenting. She changes the form of the creatures she creates. She gets her ideas from the memories of the Humans she has absorbed.

I've seen Angels and Demons...

* * * *

...It's been fifteen years now since we arrived in this sector of space. Our Mother-ship never came back...

* * * *

...I haven't aged in twenty years...

* * * *

41

Something is wrong.

I may look like Captain Jeremy Cunningham, but I know that I am not human anymore. I am not the real Jeremy Cunningham.

We are all copies of our former selves. We have lost the spark that makes us human.

There is no research going on. Half the crew has moved down to the planet.

Things are beginning to break down and we have forgotten how to fix them.

The only thing anybody is interested in is sex. We copulate all the time.

* * * *

We've lost contact with Nu-Eden. The last shuttle never came back and there is nobody left who knows how to operate the ones still in the shuttle-bays.

* * * *

The water quality in the tanks is deteriorating. The plant in the pond is dying. We haven't seen the Xandra for a long time now.

* * * *

People are changing. They are turning into monsters.

* * * *

July 20, AD 3015

This will be my last entry. I have locked myself into my quarters. When I look into the mirror I know that Captain Jeremy Cunningham is dead. He died thirty years ago. Soon I will be like the others, incoherent and without conscious thought.

A zombie.

Even now I have trouble formulating my words.

I must hurry. The station is falling apart. The upper floors are already without heat and water. It is only a matter of time until everybody is dead.

I will die with dignity, while I still have some shreds of humanity left inside me.

I may be a creature of the Xandra now, but once I was human.

Once I was Captain Jeremy Cunningham.

May God have mercy on his soul.

Chapter Eight

Commander Beringer stared at the stack of journals. He had read them a second time now. The lump in his throat was hard to swallow. Even though the Captain had only been a facsimile of his original self, he had kept his dignity right to the end. Throughout the journal he had questioned his true human identity, but he had died with his humanity still intact.

"I want to go down to the planet. If there are any Humans left down there I want to know."

"I suggest you keep your team small," Starfinder said, touching one of the journals. "Your captain described all sorts of creatures, which the Xandra created. It may be a very dangerous mission."

Beringer nodded. "I will take Lt. Wang and Starmote. Do you approve?"

"I do." Starfinder smiled. "I am surprised you chose Starmote."

"She is the logical choice." The Commander kept his voice neutral. He might have hidden motives, but he didn't elaborate. "I saw a couple of shuttles in the docking area. I hope they still work."

The space station operated again under full power. All of Beringer's marines and the rest of the Genaar had now been revived. Beringer kept his men separate from the aliens. He told Starfinder that it would be better for their morale and discipline. The alien females were very beautiful and quite seductive. He didn't want his men weakened by sexual escapades. *I want to have a fighting force that is in top condition. We don't know what awaits us on the planet.* The alien just smiled and made no comment.

"We have not detected any air traffic or any other evidence revealing whoever resides on the planet's surface possesses any form of advanced technology," Starfinder broke into his thoughts. "So the chances of you being discovered, when you arrive at night, are very slim. Have you given some thought to where exactly you want to land?"

"I think it will be the site of Alpha Colony. I've never been down to the planet's surface and I have no idea where the colony is located. Did you find anything in the data-blocks Starmote removed from the Captain's computer?"

"As a matter of fact we have." Starfinder chuckled. "Our systems are, of course, not compatible, but our computer is very sophisticated."

He held up a hand. "I am not saying yours is inferior, but I doubt if you would be able to remove and decipher data taken from our data banks."

"I am not a scientist," Beringer said. "I have no interest in why and how certain things work. Just give me a mission, a weapon and a target, and I will use any information your sophisticated computer spits out to do what must be done." He stared at Starfinder. "By the way, there must have been a lot of information in those data-blocks about Earth, our mission here and who knows what else."

"There is, but let me put your fears to rest, my friend. We will not use it against you. I've told you, we are not an aggressive species, but we may use any information we found to defend ourselves, if necessary." Starfinder smiled, but his eyes didn't. "Always remember, you invaded our station, you brought the thread of the Xandra to us. So you owe us to share any information you have discovered that may be of help. Whatever your people left behind belongs to us."

"We assumed the station abandoned," Beringer said. "Otherwise we would have built a base on one of the satellites."

"I didn't mean to criticize. I just want to put things in perspective, in case there are ever any questions about our actions or motives."

"I understand. I do trust you, and even if I didn't, do I have any choice? I am your guest and I am grateful."

Starfinder walked toward the door. Before he walked out he turned and said, "Your Captain Cunningham and I had a lot in common. He was a man of honor, and so am I. You, Commander Beringer, are a man of principles. You would never betray a friend. Neither would I. So you see there is a certain bond between us. I consider you my friend."

Beringer stared at the closing door. "I hope this friendship will never be put to the test," he murmured, shrugged and closed the log book. He almost rose from his seat, when the door slid open again and Starmote walked into the room.

"Starfinder tells me that you've chosen me to accompany you on another mission." She smiled, her dark eyes smoldering. "I thought you didn't like me."

Beringer looked at her as she stood in front in him, at the way her breasts moved under the skintight outfit when she breathed, stared for a quick moment at the slightly bulging crease between her legs. His belly tightened, a pulse began to flutter in his loins. He wanted her badly, the way he had never wanted a woman before.

"I never said that." His voice sounded hoarse in his ears. "I think you could be a valuable member of my team."

"Why would you think that? You don't know anything about me."

"Well." He managed to smile. "You've demonstrated that you know how to take care of yourself." His hand went to his chest, rubbed it.

"Are you still in pain?" she asked. "I never meant to hurt you."

"It only hurts when I breathe," he said jokingly, felt stupid when she didn't laugh. "Forget it," he said. "Don't read too much into this. To be honest, I had to take one of your people. And let's face it, you are the only choice."

"Thank you for your honesty." Her eyes flashed. "And don't worry, I won't disappoint you. When do we leave?"

"After the next sleeping period. Lt. Wang is the other member of the team. Go help him prepare the shuttle and take care of provisions. Make sure you bring a weapon."

She nodded, turned and left.

He cursed silently. He couldn't get the image of her round buttocks, the way they moved inside her body suit, out of his mind. Maybe he made a mistake to take her along. His feelings for her could compromise the whole mission. Damn it all! Why couldn't she be ugly! She wasn't even human. She was an alien.

He left his room a few moments later to check on his men. He knew they were becoming restless and bored. Morale seemed low since they learned that they were the only Humans left on the station. Some had questioned the need for keeping separated from the Genaar. Maybe it had been wrong not to give them the real reason why they were put into cryogenic suspension. He should have given them a choice.

They knew now.

All of the men were young, in top physical condition and healthy, which meant they needed sexual release.

There were more females than males among the alien crew. The Genaar females were all beautiful and made no effort to hide their sexuality. One could almost taste the pheromones they exuded.

Beringer walked through the door that led to the quarters his men occupied. Most of them sat in what they termed the 'Games Room'. There were tables and chairs, and even a viewing-sphere. Among the possessions the troopers brought with them had been a number of entertainment rods, with enough stored images to keep them entertained for years.

They switched it off when the commander entered the room, but he could still see the life-size three dimensional afterimages of the copulating man and woman who had been performing for them on the table top.

"At ease!" Beringer said, pretending not to notice. He looked around, saw the man he searched for. "Sergeant Stasnowsky, you'll be in charge while I am planet side," he said and watched the big, beefy man come to attention. A little older than most of the other marines, still a sergeant, nobody knew why and nobody knew his reasons for being here. The fact that he showed a little too much independence might have something to do with it. But everyone liked him and Beringer knew he would keep the others under control.

Beringer spoke loud enough so everybody could hear him, "I expect you to follow the Sergeant's orders and I want you all to be at constant readiness. I don't know what I'll find down there. Hopefully I'll find Humans, that is *True-Humans*. In case something goes wrong and I should not return, I have made contingency-plans. They will be made known to you at such time as is necessary." He looked at Stasnowsky. "Sergeant, meet me in two hours in my quarters for a quick briefing."

The sergeant saluted sloppily. "Yes, Sir, Commander."

Beringer's gaze fell on Lambert who had been staring at him. "Something on your mind, marine?" he asked.

Lambert, who had accompanied him on the mission to the outside, smiled thinly and hunched his shoulders forward. "Yes, there is something, Commander. Some of the men are wondering if arrangements could be made to meet with the alien women, if they are willing," he hesitated, "I mean, you yourself…"

Beringer cut him off. "*What* about me, Lambert?" he said sharply.

"Nothing, Sir." The young man clamped his mouth shut, his eyes flickered over to Sergeant Stasnowsky, who cleared his throat and said, "The men are getting nervous, they hear too many rumors. Maybe some r'n'r would boost morale."

The Commander nodded. "I'll have to talk to Starfinder. In the meantime I want everybody sharp and alert. Exercise, take cold showers, I don't care." He turned abruptly and walked out of the door. The sounds his boots made on the cold metal floor echoed down the corridor. Everything on this station looked alien, and yet, much seemed familiar.

The Genaar had developed along the same lines as the Humans. Beringer didn't know much about biology and most other sciences, but he'd be willing to bet that they wouldn't find much difference between the genetic make-ups of the two races. Interbreeding may probably be quite possible.

He admitted his attraction to Starmote, and even in the presence of the other *Genaar* females he felt a strong sexual urge. He knew his men did, too. That's why he kept them isolated.

He needed to talk to Starfinder. What made these women so attractive and irresistible? There had been plenty of beautiful women among the settlers and the crew, none of them ever caused this effect.

He glanced at his time-piece. Another gift from Starfinder, but a useful and necessary one. All of his men had received one.

The Genaar used the decimal system, they based everything on 'ten'. One day consisted of twenty *hours,* equivalent to approximately twenty-six Standard-hours.

He had some time left before his meeting with Sergeant Stasnowsky; enough time to grab something to eat. When he walked into the *kitchen,* he found himself alone. He punched up an order and waited for the three bulbs to drop onto his small tray. Beringer found the food compatible with the human digestive system, bland, but edible and nourishing, not much different from the rations he was used to. A soldier didn't, as a rule, enjoy gourmet meals.

He sighed and squeezed the contents of one of the bulbs into his mouth, winced when the strange flavor hit his taste buds.

"Enjoying your meal?"

At the sound of the voice Beringer tensed, whirled around and watched Starmote walking into the room, dressed in her usual formfitting body suit.

"You shouldn't sneak up on people like that," he said, his eyes on the deep cleft between her breasts. Her open body suit revealed more than necessary. She saw his look, smiled and went to one of the dispensers.

"I thought you were with Lieutenant Wang?" Beringer ripped off the top of another bulb. *There must be an easier way to open these damn things, besides with your teeth,* he thought. Starmote seemed to have no trouble with hers. Her teeth were white and obviously very strong.

"He was already done when I got there," she said, sucking on her bulb. Her lips were red and full, her eyes as dark as the black void of space. "Why don't you come to my quarters tonight," she said suddenly. "It might ease the tension between us."

He stared at her. "Are you serious?"

She laughed, came closer. "You Humans are a strange race. You seem to have a lot of hang-ups. You say one thing, but you mean something else. I thought you wanted to couple with me."

He felt her warm breath in his face, her lips were slightly open. Between her even teeth he saw the tip of her tongue dart like a snake in its lair. He wanted to crush his mouth against hers, loose himself in the depths of her alien eyes, run his fingers through her soft black hair. "I don't think it's a good idea," he said stiffly, hating himself for saying it, trying to still his pounding pulse. *She's offering herself,* a voice thundered in his head. *You fool! Don't blow it*!

She put a finger against his lips, shrugged her shoulders. "The offer stands. It may be our last chance to relax for awhile."

He watched her walk to the door, stood dumbfounded, stared at her plump buttocks move smoothly, enticingly, promising delicious delights.

After finishing his meal, he walked slowly out of the room and made a quick decision.

The men were still sitting in the Games Room. This time they didn't bother to shut off the viewing sphere. Two naked figures writhed on top of the table. A woman with oversized breasts had her long legs wrapped around the torso of the man she coupled with. She moved her slim body snake-like and with incredible speed underneath the over-muscled man.

They were not real. Just computer-generated images, but they seemed real, real enough to cause a reaction in Beringer.

He tore his eyes away, looked at Lambert, who had been watching him.

"Lambert," Beringer said. "I want you to pilot the shuttle. Get your gear ready. Sergeant Stasnowsky will fill you in." He turned without looking back. The harsh breathing sounds and moans of the copulating couple broke off abruptly as the door slid shut behind him.

He would talk to Starfinder about his men. They had been without female companionship far too long.

What about his own needs?

It would be easy to visit Starmote in her room. She seemed willing and waiting for him. But could he afford to get involved with her? He knew the answer to that. Anyone else, but not Starmote. She'd be under his direct command. It would violate all the rules.

He grimaced, cursed himself for being a *Man of Principles,* as Starfinder called him.

He headed back to his own quarters.

Chapter Nine

"Too many," Vienne gasped beside Viran.

Viran swung his war-hammer, ready to smash another hairless skull.

"Stop!" said a hollow voice. One of the creatures pushed his way through the crowd. Viran watched the skeletal-like figure coming toward them. The face had once been human, but not anymore, yet, the eyes shone clear in Mirtin's light. "You've done enough damage," the creature said, stumbling over the words, as if he hadn't spoken in a long time.

"I'll do more, unless you let us pass," Viran threatened, lifting his weapon. He eyed the creature. "I didn't know Zombs could talk."

"I can." The sunken eyes studied Viran. "I was like you once, strong and handsome. I had a woman who loved me. Now I am ugly and always hungry." His mouth opened to bare fangs. "I am cursed twice. I know what I turned into, unlike my brothers and sisters. They don't think, but they still feel pain. Their silent cries filled my head when you destroyed them. I felt their pain." He pointed a skeletal hand. "Go quick. I can keep back the others for a short time only."

"Why are you doing this?" Viran asked.

"Because The Mother wants it so. Even though you are not Xandra-born, you are one of The Chosen Ones. Now go!"

Viran and the women moved through the narrow opening the Zombs made for them. The stench of their rotting flesh made Viran want to retch. He gripped his hammer tight in his hand, held it in front of him. Then they were through, the light in Mirtin's hand showed the entrance to the cave. They stumbled outside, ran down a rocky trail.

"Wait," Vienne cried out. "I can't keep up."

Viran slowed down, let her catch up to him. He grinned at Mirtin, who leaned against him, holding on for support. "Your sister is weak," he said.

"She is not my sister, and I am not weak." Vienne sank to the ground, pulled off her boot and rubbed her ankle.

Mirtin directed the light at the blond girl's foot. "Are you hurt?" she asked.

"I think I sprained it."

Mirtin bent down, examined the ankle with her fingers. "It feels fine. Maybe you should take something for the pain." She fumbled in one of her pockets, pulled out an oblong device. "Unbutton."

Vienne undid the front of her shirt, slipped one side down her shoulders. Viran caught a glimpse of a small breast, noticed the smooth, white skin. Vienne saw him looking, glared at him challengingly. "Why don't you come closer so you can get a better look?"

"Oh, stop it." Mirtin put the object in her hand against Vienne's bare shoulder. "There, that should take care of it."

"Are you a healer?" Viran asked her.

"A healer?" Mirtin rose, put the object back into her pocket. "A healer, hmm…I guess in a way I am. But it is just one of my many…uh…talents."

"There is a healer in my tribe. But she is an old woman, not young and beautiful, like you."

Mirtin laughed. "Thank you. It's been a long time since a man called me beautiful and young."

Vienne rose to her feet. She closed her shirt. "He is still a savage," she hissed into Mirtin's ear, "and a man, he'll say anything to get you to spread for him."

Mirtin chuckled. "You've said it, he is a man. I happen to like men, real men."

"If we were in a different place I would not listen to your chatter," Viran growled. "We should leave here, before the Zombs decide to follow us. It is still dark. We won't be safe from them until it gets light."

"Is he in charge?" Vienne asked Mirtin.

The dark-haired girl nodded. "For now, unless you can tell us which way we should go."

"You're in command, as far as I'm concerned."

"That's good, as long as you remember that; but for now we follow Viran." Mirtin surveyed the surrounding terrain with her light. The ground looked rough and uneven. Large boulders, shrouded in fog, crouched all around them, like fat monstrosities, ready to pounce on the unwary traveler.

Vienne shivered. "I feel like a million eyes are watching us."

Viran chuckled, balanced his war-hammer in his hand. "They probably are. Anything can hide behind those rocks, or in the fog."

"Like what?" Vienne challenged him.

51

"The night spawns many creatures." Viran shrugged his massive shoulders. "Wild hounds, fire-lizards, rock-hares, night-vipers, and those are the harmless ones." He grinned, then became serious. "As long as you keep that light on we should be fairly safe from most of the creatures of the dark. But there are others."

"What a hospitable place." Vienne sighed. "One thing is certain, I know now that I should have never volunteered for this mission."

Mirtin laughed. "As if we had any choice." She touched the younger girl's shoulder. "Don't be so gloomy. We are free and have some idea of what we can expect. We'll have to find Massater and his team. That is our priority now."

"Maybe his bones are back there in that cave." Vienne said, sourly.

"I don't believe that. The report puts him farther south."

Viran listened to the women's conversation. He didn't quite understand what they discussed. A savage he might be in their eyes, but not stupid. "You are looking for a friend?" he asked. He didn't miss the warning glance Mirtin gave Vienne. "Not a friend. We don't even really know him," she explained. "He belongs to another team. He was sent to find certain rocks that we need, but we haven't heard back from him, it seems he got lost."

"Rocks? Why would you search for rocks? They are everywhere."

"Not these."

"On the island, where I live, we find rocks that our weapon maker melts to make knifes and swords. He made my war-hammer." Viran stroked the blood-spattered rough surface of his weapon. "Is that what you are looking for? Rocks to make weapons with?"

Vienne snorted. "Primitives! You can't compare that crude lump of rusty metal with the *Sirinium* we need for our converters."

"Sirinium?"

"Forget it. How can you understand!" Vienne looked at Mirtin. "Ask him, which way?"

Viran gave Mirtin a thoughtful look. "You are searching for someone, but you don't know where he is. I never asked you how you got here."

"We dropped out of the sky," Vienne from the darkness behind the older woman.

"Be silent!" Mirtin hissed, and then turned to Viran. "We were part of a caravan," she said. "When the rain started, Vienne and I became separated from the others and got lost."

"A trade caravan?" Viran said. "We sometimes trade with them."

"That's it, a trade caravan." Mirtin exhaled audibly, looked back at Vienne. "It was a trade caravan," she said over her shoulder.

Viran shook his head. A strange pair, these two. He sniffed the air. "The forest is that way," he said and pointed. "I feel safer among the trees."

With the help of Mirtin's light they had no trouble maneuvering between the big boulders. By the time they reached the forest it began to get light. Viran looked at the pink sky. "I think it will be a clear day."

They followed a well-traveled path. Viran didn't know if this happened to be the same path the Zombs used. It didn't matter. He wanted to get as far away from their lair as possible. Later he would decide what direction to take.

The sun stood high in the sky when they crossed a small creek. Viran dropped to his belly, drank from the clear, cool water. When he looked up, he saw Mirtin crouching beside him. She dipped a flexible tube into the water. The tube ended in a small gourd with another tube coming out on top. Mirtin sucked on it.

"What a strange way to drink water," he commented.

"It might be contaminated. We don't want to get sick." Mirtin said.

Viran laughed. "The water will not make you sick, but without it you will surely die."

After Vienne had taken her fill in the same peculiar manner, they walked on. The path ended in a large clearing. It didn't surprise Viran to see the pond. He looked down at himself, at the crusted mud and blood that covered his body. "I am taking a bath," he announced. He stripped off his trousers and dove naked into the dark water. When he came up for air, he became aware of the large plant floating in the middle of the pond. Looking back to shore he saw the two women step out of their clothes and slowly walk to the edge of the pond.

Watching them, he found Mirtin the more voluptuous one of the two, with her large and full breasts and her wide, smooth hips. Below her flat belly a thick, black triangle covered her pubic area.

Vienne was taller than Mirtin, but thin, her breasts small, like the ones of a girl barely out of puberty. Between her extremely long, slim legs her pubic hair seemed almost non-existent, exposing her slit to Viran's eyes. Looking at her, he felt a strange attraction. She reminded him a little of Angela, the winged girl.

He began rubbing the dirt off his body, feeling better already.

"Don't go near that plant!" he called out a warning as they began swimming toward the giant floating plant.

"Why not?" Mirtin asked, treading water.

"It eats people."

Viran laughed when Vienne gave a little shriek and headed back to shore. She stopped, not far away from him, crossed her arms over her breasts. "What is so funny?'

"You." He chuckled. "Don't worry. You have nothing to fear during the day. Night is a different story. Don't you know anything?"

"I know plenty. And stop staring at me!"

"Not much to stare at," Viran mumbled and ducked under the water. His eyes were open; he saw an oblong shape heading toward Vienne. It attached itself to her belly and flowed down to her genitals.

He surfaced in front of the young woman and watched the change in her face.

Her hands cupped her small breasts, rubbed them. She stared at Viran, her blue eyes large, her lips slightly apart. Reaching for his hand, she pulled him onto the dry land, pushed him onto his back and straddled him. Her hands went down to find his penis, began fondling it.

He reacted swiftly, and then she sank into his lap. His stiff penis slid into creamy softness. He groaned when the pleasure began surging through his body. She seemed out of control, her thin body undulating fiercely above him. Her small buttocks squirmed in his big hands as he tried to steady her. Lunging up, he entered her deeply. His hands grabbed her hips and held her down as he erupted inside her.

She screamed, her eyes and lips wide open, her small breasts taut and slick with a mixture of water and perspiration. He pulled her down. Licking her breasts, he tasted her salty skin. His lips moved along her neck, fastened on her mouth. She returned his kiss hungrily, snapped her lower body against his, demanding his attention. He rolled her over. She bent her legs and he moved between her widespread thighs. Squirming underneath him, she dug her fingers painfully into his biceps. When he freed her mouth to gasp for air, a loud cry escaped her lips.

He looked into her blue eyes. They were unfocused, as if looking at something far away, but not at him. She climaxed numerous times. When he felt his own orgasm approaching, he waited until she quivered in his arms again, then he let the thunderous pleasure roll over him.

They both finished simultaneously, he pulled out, rolled onto his back, his breath ragged in his throat.

Beside him Vienne gasped for air. He felt her get up after awhile. Moments later he heard the splash of water as she dove into it.

Without looking, he knew what she had to do. It didn't surprise him, when he saw the silhouette of Mirtin above him. She said nothing, just straddled him. He looked at the thick black triangle between her legs and watched it touch the tip of his erect organ. Slowly, she swallowed him into her. They both cried out when the waves of pleasure washed through their bodies.

Her gray eyes were on his face as she began to rotate her hips. Reaching up he put his hands over her ample breasts and squeezed gently. They said nothing to each other, but their eyes were locked the whole time. Only when he began pumping his discharge into her, did she lift her head, a series of short cries emitted from her open mouth. Then she collapsed on top of him, lay gasping for air in his strong arms. After awhile she kissed him on the lips and squirmed out of his grasp.

He watched her walk into the water and watched her peel off the thin gelatin film from her pubic area. She ducked under water, shook herself when she surfaced again. Then she came back slowly, a thoughtful look on her face.

He studied her body when she stood beside him, dripping water. She had a good figure, lovely, full breasts. Her nipples stood rigid from the cool water.

She knelt down, staring at his half-erect penis. "I don't understand what just happened," she said in a low voice.

Viran grinned. "We copulated. Don't tell me you've never done it before."

"Of course I have." She managed a smile. "I'm not saying I didn't like it. You're a handsome young man, and I am attracted to you, but the way it happened...the unbelievable pleasure..." She looked at Vienne, who sat brooding in the grass a few steps away. "She is a surprise."

Viran turned his head to look at the blond young woman. "I knew she had fire inside her, but she even surprised me," he chuckled.

Vienne glared at him. "I hope I am not going to carry your bastard child," she said gloomily.

Viran laughed. "My seed never entered your womb. It is the Xandra who will make use of it."

"Who is the Xandra?" Mirtin asked.

"She is The Mother. Most of the creatures in this world were created by her."

"You too?"

Viran shook his head. "I am a True-Human, born by a real woman." He gave Mirtin a speculating look. "It seems very strange that you are so ignorant about the basic things in life. The place you come from must certainly be far away from all civilization."

Shrill laughter from Vienne made him stare at her. "*Far from civilization*, he says." She doubled over with hysterical laughter.

"What's with her?" Viran asked, puzzled.

"She is upset. You're the first man she ever made love to. She doesn't like men."

"I didn't *make love* to him." Vienne said with a loud voice. "We coupled like two animals in heat. We fucked. It was disgusting."

"You seemed to enjoy it," Mirtin said.

Vienne glared at her. "That is what is so disgusting." She rose to her feet, stumbled closer, dropped to her knees beside Viran and stared at his penis. "And I want more of it. I've never experienced such intense pleasure." Her hand reached out, her fingers curled around Viran's organ and squeezed it. Like a snake, it moved in her hand, grew until it became stiff and solid. With a loud moan, Vienne straddled Viran and guided the thick pole between her legs.

Viran watched in surprise as his sex-organ disappeared inside the young woman's belly. Before the shockwaves rolled over him, he became briefly aware of the glittering film covering Vienne's pubic area and inner thighs. Then he lost himself again in a world of nearly unbearable pleasure.

Inside his head he heard silent laughter. A beautiful woman with flaming hair and black liquid eyes came to him out of the fog that filled his mind. His eyes were on Vienne, but they didn't see her. The ghostly body of the Xandra enveloped the girl like a transparent cloak. Long red hair fluttered in a nonexistent breeze. *I will be part of you forever* echoed her words through his mind.

He pushed upwards, cried out when his seed erupted from him.

Chapter Ten

The image of Nu-Eden filled most of the screen. Part of the planet lay in darkness. Soon the shuttle would enter the atmosphere and descent rapidly toward the surface. Their destination lay in the southern part of the huge landmass that stretched around most of the northern half of the planet. An ocean a thousand kilometers wide separated the southern continent from its northern counterpart. It narrowed to about two hundred kilometers where two tongues of land tried to touch.

Commander Beringer leaned back in his seat. He saw Lambert, who piloted the shuttle, do the same, for lack of anything else to do. They had programmed the co-ordinates of Alpha-Colony into the shuttle's computer and the auto-pilot would bring them safely down, better than any human pilot could do.

Beringer looked at Starmote, who sat across from him. She didn't wear her tight body-suit. Instead she opted for a loose-fitting camouflage outfit with lots of pockets. Not unlike the outfits the Humans wore.

She saw his look and smiled, her dark eyes hidden behind her lowered long lashes. Even in these loose clothes she looked good.

Even though he didn't see any weapons, he knew she was armed.

He had his own laser-pistol strapped to his hip, preferring to have it in plain sight. Just a little bit of extra insurance.

Lt. Wang, who sat beside Starmote, had his eyes closed. Beringer knew that he wasn't sleeping. Probably meditating.

A slight shudder went through the shuttle as the planet's atmosphere protested against the intruder. Stabilizers cut in and cooling coils under the outer shell neutralized the heat caused by friction. Beringer saw the tops of tall trees on the screen. Then the view changed to show tree-trunks, shrubbery and a small body of water inside a large clearing.

The shuttle had landed.

They scanned for larger life-forms in the immediate area, but the results were negative.

"I guess it is safe," Beringer said and nodded to Lt. Wang who got up and gave the command to open the exit door. It slid open. Cool, humid air entered the cabin. Beringer took a deep breath, detected an unfamiliar sweet odor.

"Filters!" he said sharply and pulled up the small flesh-colored mask that hung under his chin, fitted it over his nose.

Lt. Wang took the first step outside. The Commander followed next, with Starmote close behind him. Lambert stayed in the shuttle.

Beringer looked around. His eyes adjusted to the semi-darkness. When he looked up, he saw the reddish disk of one of the three moons. All seemed quiet, except for the monotonous drumming of a night creature.

"Seal the shuttle," he told Lambert over the com-link in his earlobe and watched the door slide shut. Lambert had his orders, no need to tell him more.

Enough light from the satellite let them see the path that led through the clearing. Starmote studied a small disk she had strapped to her wrist. "Our destination lies in that direction," she said, pointing. She took the lead. Beringer followed her after looking one more time at the still water of the pond. He saw the large plant floating in its center. He knew what it represented and shuddered.

Lt. Wang fell in behind him. Beringer noticed that he had drawn his laser-pistol.

Low vegetation covered the path they followed. Whatever large animal had made it obviously didn't use it very much.

"According to the map it should take us a little over one hour to get there," Starmote said.

Beringer knew that she had not said *hour,* but that's how the implanted device translated it. Lt. Wang had been outfitted with his own translator, eliminating any problems with communication between them. None of the other soldiers back on the station had been given a translator, except for Sergeant Stasnowsky.

Beringer almost bumped into Starmote. She stood, listening, then reached into one of her large pockets and pulled out a pair of night-goggles.

Beringer became aware that the trees had become taller, their trunks and branches thicker. The light from the moon did not penetrate the dense foliage, leaving the path in semi-darkness.

"I thought I heard something moving above us," Starmote said, looking up.

A shrill, gurgling sound nearby made Beringer reach for his gun. Behind him Lt. Wang fell into a crouch, scanned the thick undergrowth. Starmote used her search light to illuminate the surrounding forest. A small lizard-like creature jumped up, scurried away.

"You're not used to this king of thing, are you, Commander?" Starmote made another sweep with her light. Then she clicked it back into her belt.

"I prefer a war-ship and the vastness of space." Beringer holstered his gun. "I trust a ship's instruments more than my own senses."

"If it makes you feel any better, I am not very fond of this dense growth myself. I feel trapped. There is no way to run."

Beringer smiled grimly. "I'm quite relieved to hear that, Starmote. Now I feel really safe. Let's move on."

Alpha-Colony proved to be a disappointment. They only found abandoned buildings. One of the structures looked like a place of worship. The part that still stood, actually quite well preserved, had been built from pre-fab materials. The rooms they added later consisted of nothing but decaying ruins, just heaps of crumbling clay bricks. Creeping vines and slippery moss covered most of the walls and roofs.

"Looks like a once thriving community," Beringer said. "Wonder why they abandoned it." He removed his filter-mask and inhaled the fresh morning air.

Lt. Wang checked out one of a number of small metal structures. "These must be the original pre-fab buildings the first colonists put up," he said as he entered the small metal shed. Beringer could hear his voice clearly over his communicator.

"This one looks like a power station, but it has been stripped," the lieutenant's voice came from inside the shed.

There were ruins of other dwellings, most of them built from clay bricks or stones. If there ever had been any roads the forest claimed them a long time ago. Only a narrow path made by some animal wound its way through the ruins.

A sharp cracking sound, like an explosion, brought Lt. Wang running out of the shed, his weapon in his hand. "What was that?" he inquired.

Two more sharp cracks in quick succession, then the wailing scream of a woman.

"It's coming from that direction," Starmote said and began running down the path, Beringer and the lieutenant close behind her. The forest ended, before them lay an open grass-covered valley. They stopped at the edge of the forest and hid behind the thick tree-trunks.

Beside a small river that snaked through the valley stood a number of tents. They saw figures moving among the tents. Some looked like large animals with men on their backs.

"Those are horses," Beringer whispered to Lt. Wang. He pulled out a pair of distance goggles, slipped them over his eyes. The image he focused on zoomed in, became clear and made him curse.

The men riding the horses were Humans, scruffy looking, with bearded faces and filthy, torn clothing. What they carried in their hands were clearly rifles. One of the men pointed it at a figure running away. Beringer heard the explosive sound as the rifle discharged, and then he saw the victim stumble and collapse.

"Projectile weapons," Starmote said beside Beringer. "Primitive, but effective."

"They kill like any other weapon!" Beringer cursed. "It's a massacre down there. We'll have to stop it."

"Appearances can be deceiving." Starmote said.

"I agree." Lt. Wang slipped off his goggles. "We don't know who the good guys are."

The crack of a rifle and falling of another body made up Beringer's mind. "It is obvious to me who the killers are. They must be stopped." He stepped out from behind the trees and began walking in the direction of the camp. "Keep your weapon holstered," he told his lieutenant. "Same goes for you, Starmote, where ever you carry yours."

When they came closer to the cluster of tents, Beringer saw bodies lying on the ground. A group of what appeared to be naked women were huddled together near one of the tents. One of the riders had dismounted, stood in front of them.

There were six riders. Bandits, as far as Beringer was concerned. One of them noticed the commander and his group approaching, wheeled his mount around and came galloping toward them. The horse, a black stallion, reared up on its hind legs when the rider pulled hard on the leather reins.

"If he is trying to impress us, he's succeeded," Lt. Wang said beside Beringer. "I've seen live horses before, but this one is huge."

"The horse isn't dangerous, but its owner is," Beringer said with a low voice.

"Who are you?" demanded the man on top of the horse to know. He spoke with a harsh, gravelly voice. The rifle in his hand pointed at the Commander.

Beringer studied the weapon casually and suppressed a smug smile. He'd never seen a rifle like this one before, except in a military museum. A thousand years out of date. No, he corrected himself, two thousand years. A black powder rifle that fired only one bullet at a time, and probably quite inaccurate. Of course, from a distance like this as deadly as any other weapon.

"We are travelers," Beringer said, keeping an eye on the man's rifle-hand.

The man's eyes were hidden under thick, black eyebrows. A scruffy black beard covered his mouth, but by the way he spoke made it evident that he didn't have any front teeth. "What is your business here?" he asked.

"It depends on your answer." Beringer stared at the man. "Why are you murdering these people?"

"People? They're not people, they are *Xandra*. We are bounty hunters. We are just putting them out of their misery." He looked at Starmote, then back at Beringer. "That one is not human, looks *Xandra*. What about you and the other one? You're both without beards. Maybe you are *Xandra-born*, too."

"I am human," Beringer said coldly. "But I'm not sure that you are."

The other man let out a barking laugh, motioned with his rifle. "Go, I want you to meet the Sniffer, he'll know if you're a True-Human. "

Beringer counted six men on horses and the one who stood in front of the women. All the lifeless bodies on the ground were men, clean-shaven, dressed in brown robes.

"This one objects to our shooting these vermin," announced the man behind Beringer. His companions howled with laughter.

"Maybe he's got good reason," one of them said, glaring at Starmote with open hostility. "That one looks *Xandra*."

"The Sniffer will tell us."

The one they called the *Sniffer* sat inside a small, covered wagon. His white beard reached almost down to his navel. A white robe that had seen better days covered his scrawny frame. He climbed down from his wagon and stared at Beringer out of bright blue eyes. "Let me smell your breath," he said with a high-pitched voice. When the Commander exhaled into his face, the Sniffer scratched his balding head.

"He doesn't smell bad," he said to the man who had brought them. "But he doesn't small like a *Xandra-born* creature. I don't know." He gazed at Starmote. "You--blow in my face."

Starmote took a deep breath and blew hard.

"Hey, hey," the Sniffer screeched, "not so hard. Gently! Like this." He breathed against Starmote's face.

She pulled away and coughed. "You smell like a carrion-eater," she gasped.

"I'm a True-Human. Nobody will ever mistake me for a *Xandra-born*. Now, breathe at me!"

Starmote let him smell her breath. He inhaled deeply, looked into her large, black eyes. "You have the eyes of a *Nymph,* but don't behave like one. I know you are a female, even if you dress like a man. Your voice is too soft. Let's see your breasts."

Starmote hesitated for a moment and looked back at Beringer. He nodded slightly. She shrugged, opened the front of her baggy shirt and let her naked breasts tumble out. Beringer stared at their white, creamy perfection, felt a stab of anger when he heard the watching men groan.

The Sniffer licked his lips. "I must suck one," he said, his squeaky voice cracking. He took one thick, long nipple into his mouth and sucked. Starmote pulled away. "That's enough!" she snapped.

"Nothing," the Sniffer said. "She doesn't taste like a *Nymph.* "

"I say we kill them," said one of the watching men. "They don't look right to me."

Beringer noticed that Lt. Wang had moved toward the edge of the circle the riders formed around them. His hand hovered close to his laser.

"I agree, let's kill them," said the one who had spotted them first. He slid off his horse, stepped up to Starmote, leered at her. "But first I'll have some fun with this one." He reached out toward her and let out a gurgling scream, fell back, clutching his throat. Red blood welled through his fingers. Starmote moved already toward one of the riders, reached up to pull him off his horse.

Beringer drew his weapon, barely managed to throw himself to one side to avoid being trampled by one of the horses. He saw a rifle-butt descent, fired his laser into a man's chest. As he whirled to look for another opponent, he saw Lt. Wang facing one of the rogues who swung a broad sword in front of him. Wang brought up his laser and shot the man in the head. He fell without a sound, impaling himself on his own sword.

The man Starmote pulled off his horse lay in a crumpled heap on the ground. Starmote swung herself on the horse. She kept the reins tight to keep it from bolting away. One of the remaining two mounted riders lifted his rifle and aimed it at Starmote. Beringer's laser drilled a hole into his skull, frying the brain inside.

The last of the mounted bandits tried to ride down Lt. Wang, but Wang spun away and killed the man with a burst form his laser.

Watching Wang in action confirmed again the reason why Beringer had chosen him to be part of this team.

Two men were still alive, the Sniffer and the one who had been guarding the women. The latter wasn't there anymore. When Beringer searched for him, he saw a horse and a rider hightailing it halfway down the valley. Beringer turned toward the old man, who stood petrified beside his wagon, eyes wide.

"What are you?" The Sniffer's voice was quaking with fear.

"We are Humans, real Humans," Beringer told him.

"You can't be human. You must be gods or demons. I saw the lightning bolts that killed my companions."

Starmote walked up to him, slapped him across the face. "That's for sucking on my breast," she said, slapping him again. "And that's for breathing on me. I should kill you."

"Oh, please, no, I am just an innocent traveler. They forced me to accompany them," the old man whined, then spit into the trampled grass. "They are nothing to me. You did me a favor by killing them and setting me free."

Beringer looked around at the carnage they had caused. Six men dead in a matter of seconds. Then his gaze traveled to the tents. He saw the bodies of the ones the dead men murdered. His eyes fell on the group of naked women. They all looked young. Young and beautiful.

They saw his look and stared back at him out of large, fearful eyes. When he began walking toward them, they cowered down, pressing close together. "Don't kill us, please," one of them pleaded when he stood in front of them. He smiled grimly, hating the men who had caused them such terror. "You have nothing to fear from us," he said gently. "Why would I want to kill you?"

"Because we are of the *Xandra,*" the young woman said.

"You look human to me."

"They say we have no soul. That's why they hate us. But we have feelings, just like them. We are not animals and we are not evil." The young woman lifted her chin in defiance. "We worship the Xandra, she is our mother and she teaches us not to hate, but to love. Is that evil?"

"That is the philosophy of the Genaar, too," Starmote said softly beside Beringer.

Beringer looked at her, as she stood beside him, spattered blood covering her face and clothing, even her exposed white breasts.

"Yours, too?" he asked, admiring her fierce beauty, loving her more than ever.

"Not mine," she said.

Chapter Eleven

Viran squinted at the bright sun as it slowly dipped toward the tree tops, then he glanced at Vienne. She sat cross legged on top of a large stone that looked out of place in the high grass. Munching on a handful of berries she had picked, she seemed to study him. "You're sure these are not poisonous?" she asked.

Viran chuckled. "You might get a little amorous if you eat too many."

She stopped eating. "What do you mean by that?"

He shrugged, grinned. "You'll see."

Mirtin laughed, stroked Viran's arm. "Maybe I ate too many of them. I feel a little strange in my belly." She leaned over and nibbled on his ear, her hand touched the inside of his thigh. She giggled when she noticed the movement of his penis.

Vienne snorted loudly. "You two go right ahead, I don't care. I won't have any of that again." She threw away the rest of her berries.

"You don't like me very much," Viran said to her.

She averted her eyes when she spoke. "I didn't in the beginning, but I don't know what happened to me. Now I…" she hesitated, then she looked at him, "now I desire you. Just thinking of having you inside me makes me tingle all over." She put her face into her hands, began to sob uncontrollably.

Viran shook his head, perplexed. "Why is she crying?" he asked Mirtin.

The dark haired woman shrugged. "She is probably very confused. As I told you before, she doesn't like men."

"How can a woman not like men? That is the natural order of things."

"I guess you don't understand what I'm talking about. She likes women."

"She likes women? What kind of nonsense is that? A woman can't couple with another woman."

Mirtin chuckled. "You'd be surprised what women can do. But let's not talk about what Vienne likes, let's talk about what I like, and I like this." Her fingers curled around his erection. When he entered her he realized that she didn't go to the pond to get a seed pouch. He smiled. The Xandra did not cause her desire for him. She did it, because she wanted him.

The coupling with her differed this time, not intense and furious, but almost gentle. She didn't act wild and fierce as before, but still with great passion. When he erupted inside her, she cried out, held him close. His own orgasm did not seem to rip his insides apart, they were the way he remembered them when he coupled with the girls on the island.

She smiled and kissed him.

He pulled out of her, rolled onto his back. The sun had disappeared behind the trees. It would be getting dark soon.

"We have to look for some shelter," he said. "It is not good to travel in the night." He rose to his feet, pulled on his trousers, then his boots. He saw Vienne watching him. She still sat in the same position on top of the rock. "Get dressed," he told her, "it will get cold."

She didn't move immediately, just sat there, looking at him. She chewed on her lower lip. Then she slid off the rock, ran toward the pond. With a loud splash she dove into the water, disappeared. When she came back out, she walked slowly toward Viran, a strange, dreamy look on her face.

She stood in front of him, looked up into his eyes. "Take off your pants," she said in a dreamy voice and began to undo his belt. Viran looked down at her glistening naked body. She pushed out her small breasts. He noticed the erect nipples. He didn't believe the cold water caused it.

Her red lips were open and her breath was coming faster. "Hurry," she gasped, "don't just stand there, take them off!"

He let her push down his pants, stepped out of his boots. Then she pushed him backwards onto the ground. He watched her mount him, watched her hairless sex-organ descent onto his erect penis. He saw the shiny thin film that covered her genitals, belly and inner thighs. When her puffy vaginal lips closed on the tip of his organ, he moaned and lunged up, entered her deeply. The fire raced through his body, touched his mind.

His hands clamped onto her small, conical breasts, squeezed them. She moved furiously in his lap, pumped her slim hips with ever increasing speed. Again he saw the vision of the woman with the flaming hair. She laughed silently as her ghostly body rode him in unison with Vienne.

When he erupted, Vienne's body accepted his seeds, but he saw the voluptuous body and beautiful face of the Xandra. He knew that, even though he spilled his seeds into Vienne, it was really the Xandra who received his gift. The seed-pouch that covered the insides of Vienne's sex-tube kept Viran's seeds from entering the young woman's womb.

It would not be Vienne who would bear a child. His seed would grow inside the seed-pouch. Once the child reached the full grown stage, the pod would split open to give birth to another Xandra-human.

Aware of this fact, Viran didn't question it. This was the way of life. He would have no attachment to his offspring.

His eyes focused on Vienne's sweat-drenched body. The soft walls of her sex-sheath still pulsating around his shaft, she milked him with gentle force, her lips open and her eyes closed.

Viran noticed that the light, which bathed her body, came from the two wanderers who had climbed into the night sky and he realized that they had copulated for a very long time. His body felt suddenly tired.

Vienne opened her eyes and seemed to come out of the trance she had been in. She looked at Viran, and then looked down at their joined bodies. Slowly, she lifted up and watched as his organ slipped out of her. Without a word, she rose and walked to the pond. She stood at the edge for a moment. Then she waded into the water and began washing her body. Her hands removed the thin, opaque film from her genitals, rolled it into a ball and let it slide into the water.

Viran watched her come back out. She walked past him without looking at him, picked up her clothes and dressed. "It is chilly," she said to Mirtin who had been watching her also. Vienne went close to Mirtin, who wrapped her arms around her. Mirtin looked at Viran. "We should rest," she said.

He nodded, walked up to the two women. "It is too late to look for shelter now, we'll stay here. There is some protection under that tree."

The women followed him. The tree was tall, with a thick trunk and low hanging branches. They crawled into the small cave the branches and roots formed.

"I am cold," Vienne said with a small voice. Her clothes were damp. Mirtin and Viran lay down on either side of her. Again Viran felt regret that he did not have his cape. It would have helped to keep the chill away. Even though naked from above the waist, he didn't feel cold. He suffered through colder nights on the island.

They slept. When Viran awoke, he found Vienne snuggled against him, her arm thrown across his broad chest. He heard the small morning creatures shriek in the tree-tops. The sun would come up soon.

The fluttering sound of a pair of great wings made him crane his neck to search the open sky above him. Then he saw the silhouette of an angel outlined against the reddish sky. She descended swiftly, landed on soft feet beside the tree.

"Viran," she said with a sweet smile. "I see you didn't miss me too much."

Mirtin and Vienne opened their eyes at the sound of the voice. Mirtin stared at the crouching winged girl. "Who is that?" she asked.

"This is Angela," Viran said. "She's a friend."

Vienne sat up and rubbed the sleep from her eyes. "She has wings," she said with a startled voice.

"You've never seen an angel?" Viran asked.

"Not in the flesh." Vienne pinched herself. "Is this all a bad dream or am I dead? Maybe we crashed and I died."

The winged girl laughed. "You have peculiar friends, Viran."

Viran smiled. "They're strangers. There is much they don't seem to know. But I've grown fond of them."

Vienne let out a strangled laugh. "He's fond of us! Did you hear that, Mirtin? The savage is fond of us. But why should I be surprised, after he probably gave both of us a child."

"Oh, Vienne." Mirtin looked at her in surprise. "Last night you couldn't get enough of him and today you call him a savage."

Vienne shook her head. "I can't explain what happened last night. Most of it is a blur, and, please, don't tell me about it, I don't think I want to know."

"She's crazy about me," Viran said to the winged girl, a smirk on his face.

Angela smiled. "She's beautiful." A frown ran through her fine features. "You probably gave her what you would like to give to me, but she does not seem happy. This is a paradox. She is sad and I am sad, but both of us for different reason." She knelt and touched Viran's arm. "The Xandra sends a message: Tread carefully. Remember, I will be with you, always." She looked into Viran's eyes. "I don't know what it means."

"How did you find me?" Viran asked.

Angela shrugged her slim shoulders. "The Mother has chosen you as her champion. She knows where you are at all times. When she lay with you she put part of herself inside you."

"How can that be? I am not *Xandra-born*."

"The Great Mother can do many things. It is true, you were born of a woman. That is the reason she chose you, Viran, to be her eyes and ears in places where she cannot be." The girl bent close to him, touched his cheek and kissed him on the lips. "I wish you well," she whispered. She rose on light feet, spread her wings and jumped into the air. She hovered for a moment, and then she lifted herself above the trees and disappeared.

"This place is full of strange beings," Mirtin said. "It doesn't make sense. So many different life-forms." She frowned, giving Viran a thoughtful look. "Tell me more about this Xandra. Who is she? That winged girl called her *The Great Mother*."

"That is so because she is the mother of most of the creatures in this world."

"Is she a goddess? Do you pray to her?"

"She is a goddess, some pray to her. I don't."

"I see. So she is not real."

Viran laughed. "Oh, she is quite real. As real as you and I."

"How do you know? Have you ever seen her?"

"I've seen her." Viran looked past Mirtin. His thoughts took him back to the temple. "She is the most beautiful woman I ever saw. She gives pleasures beyond imagination. I cannot get her out of my mind."

Mirtin shook him. "You make no sense, Viran. If she is flesh and blood then she can't be a goddess." Mirtin looked at Vienne. "We'll have to find out more. This Xandra is a power we have to reckon with. She could be dangerous. When I was briefed I was told about a supernatural being they call *Mother of Light.* She apparently lives in a temple in the only large city we found. We don't know if she is real or just an idol."

"The Xandra calls herself Mother of Light," Viran said.

"You say you've seen her. Were you at her temple in the City?"

"I've never been to the City, but I've heard of it. I was with the Xandra in one of the old places where people used to worship her." Viran was thoughtful. "She called me to her. She said she chose me to father her children."

Vienne laughed. "Looks like even here these women ply their trade. And men are so gullible they'll stick their horn into any woman who will spread her legs. They'll even call her a goddess if she tells them she is one. I don't believe in supernatural beings."

"Be quiet, Vienne," Mirtin told her. "You have to learn to be more subtle." She turned back to Viran. "Where does the Xandra live?"

Viran pointed to the pond. "She lives in the water. She lives in the Xandra-plant."

"She lives inside that plant? Is she a water-creature?"

Viran tried to be patient, but didn't find it easy. "She does not live in the plant, she is the plant."

"A sentient plant," Mirtin mused, "an intelligent plant that lives in the water, hmm, that's interesting."

"She doesn't live in the water, she is the water." Viran said.

Mirtin threw up her hands. "You're loosing me, Viran. Damn it, it is so hard to get past these superstitions. She is a plant, but she is also the water, she is a beautiful woman, she is a goddess. What the hell is she?"

Viran smiled patiently. "She is all that and more. Some say she is good, some say she is evil. Some worship her, some fear her. She is neither and she is both."

"I give up. Tell me one more thing. Yesterday, from what I remember, there was this transparent mass that molded itself over mine and Vienne's genitals. You said we wouldn't get pregnant because of it. Explain."

"Those are seed-pouches. The Xandra-plant produces them. Females put them on their bellies. The pouches catch the male's seeds. The seeds grow inside the pouch, just like in a woman's belly, only faster. When the pod splits open a fully grown man or woman is born. But they're not real Humans, that's why we call them Xandra-born."

"You've mentioned them before. That is almost impossible to believe. When the seed-pouch attaches itself to a host, it probably injects some kind of aphrodisiac into the host's system. That is why we acted so crazy." She put a hand on Vienne's arm. "There is your explanation, Blue-eyes. You were drugged." She stared at the floating giant plant in the pond. "You warned us not to get near it, you said, it eats people. What did you mean by that, Viran?"

"The plant eats people and other creatures," Viran said, "but only at night. I've never seen it happen. The Xandra does not live on my island. It is too cold. Most of what I told you was told to me by my teacher, Orin."

Vienne smirked. "So it's all heresy. Go trust a savage to tell you a good story."

"You call me a savage," Viran said to her, "but it is you who is ignorant of the way things are. Mirtin tells me that you prefer women to men. Sometimes among my people a girl is born who suffers from that sickness, but she is usually cured from it the first time she lies with a man. If she isn't then she is outcast. Women were born to be mothers. They cannot become mothers unless they couple with a man. That is the way it was intended. Anything else is an abomination of nature. A woman does not lie down with a woman and neither does a man with another man."

"You are an ignorant, insolent savage and a bastard," Vienne said with a low voice. "I am not an abomination. On my world there are no men, they all died from a mysterious disease shortly after it was colonized. We had no contact with the rest of the galaxy, since we were so far away from the usual exploration routes. If we wanted to flourish we had to find a way to have children. So we did. When the first children were born they were all females and it has been like that for generations. When we made contact again, our way of life was established, and it may never change. So don't call me a freak of nature, you, who couples with a plant!"

Mirtin put a hand on Vienne's shoulder. "You talk too much, Blue-eyes," she said gently, "fortunately he won't understand a thing you just said."

Vienne shrugged off Mirtin's hand. "I don't care. I hate this awful place and I want to get off it. I was never meant for this kind of work." She rose to her feet and ran toward the pond.

Viran watched her as she shed her clothing and stood naked at the edge of the pond. Contrary to what Mirtin had said, he had understood what Vienne had told him. He felt sorry for her. How could you live in a place where there were no men? Who would do the hunting? Who would protect the women against predators?

He wanted to take her into his arms and hold her. She seemed so soft and helpless, the way she stood there looking into the water. He thought of the women on the island, of Gilda, Sinda, and Nelly. They were different. Big and strong, not fragile and beautiful, like Vienne.

The sun appeared over the tree-tops, bathing the girl with a golden light. Looking at her slim graceful form and her small round buttocks, he experienced a sudden throbbing in his loins.

The touch of Mirtin's warm hand on his arm made him turn to look at her.

Mirtin smiled. "You desire her," she said softly. "I can see it in your eyes. Why is it that men always want what they cannot have? Don't you know how I feel about you?"

"I cannot see into your heart," Viran said. "Last night you coupled with me because you desired me. You did not need the seed-pouch. But what do you see in me? Do you see *me* or do you see just a man who is available. I know that you admire my physical body, as I admire yours and Vienne's. You are both beautiful, but so is the Xandra."

Mirtin looked into his eyes. "For a savage you possess extremely deep insights. You are right, I admire your body and your animal-physique. It turns me on. I might even get to love you. Who knows?"

She kissed him gently on the lips. "I am hungry," she said, "maybe you can find us something to eat."

Chapter Twelve

The sun hung like a ball of hot fire in the sky. Its bright light illuminated the path they were on. Viran inhaled the warm, humid air and let it fill his lungs. It was so different here on the mainland. Back on the island the air was always crisp and quite dry. His body slick with perspiration, he wondered why the two women did not sweat like him.

"It's the clothing we wear," Mirtin explained when he asked. "It acts like an insulator against cold and heat."

He didn't quite understand it, but he nodded. His own leather breeches were plastered against his skin, and his feet felt hot in his boots.

"Is it always this warm here?" Vienne asked.

"Not always, but most of the time."

"Last night I was cold," Vienne said. "Where I come from it is much warmer, but not so humid."

"It's a desert." Mirtin chuckled. "I've been there. I don't know how your people ever survived."

"I admit, it is quite barren in some regions, but we do have nice places." Vienne said defiantly. "I feel homesick."

Viran stopped walking, held up a hand. "I hear voices. I think there are people ahead."

They walked on slowly and with caution. The trail stopped abruptly, the forest seemed to have ended. Ahead of them lay a grassy area, with groves of trees spattered throughout. In the far distance they could see the white tops of snow-covered mountains.

"This is beautiful," Vienne exclaimed. "And so peaceful."

Not far from them glistened a small lake, beside it a cluster of tents. Viran could see the covered wagons the trade caravans used. Their animals grazed nearby.

Mirtin studied the tents through a device she put in front of her eyes. "They're human," she said. "Are they friendly?"

"They're traders." Viran shaded his eyes. "Maybe they can tell us where we are." He began walking toward the small camp. The women followed him with apprehension. Viran knew that they had been spotted, but nobody seemed to take much notice of them. The traders were, as a rule, peaceful. Some would be True-Humans, some Xandra-born. Usually the women were Xandra-born. He didn't know why.

Probably because there would be no offspring. Traders didn't like small children. They'd be a burden on the trail.

Viran stopped beside one of the tents. A man sat by a small fire, roasting a bird on a stick. "Who is your trail-master?" Viran asked him. The man looked up, fixed his eyes on Viran. Then he looked at the two women, letting his gaze linger on Mirtin.

"*Your* women?" the man asked.

Viran smiled, shook his head. "No, I'm their guide."

"Why do you want to see the trail-master?"

"We're lost," Mirtin said.

The man smirked, pulled the charred bird out of the fire and tested it with one finger. "I guess you hired the wrong guide," he commented and gave Mirtin a calculating look. "Maybe you want to join us. We're on the way to the City."

"Maybe." Mirtin shrugged. She glanced at Vienne. "It might be a good idea. There is safety in numbers."

"There might be." Vienne sounded dubious. "But are we safe from him? You know what he wants."

The tent flap behind the man flew open, a dark haired woman stuck out her head. She gave Mirtin an inquiring look. "Is he trying to persuade you to join him? Forget it, he's already taken."

The man laughed good-humoredly. "That's my woman. Don't mind her." He ripped a piece of meat out of the bird's breast, bit into it.

The woman stared at Viran. "Do these females belong to you? They look strange. Are they *Xandra*?"

"Are you?" Viran countered.

She pushed out her chest. Viran could see her nipples poking against the coarse robe she wore. "I'm woman-born," she said proudly. "I am with child."

The man grunted. "That's why I need another woman. What am I going to do with a little one? You'll have to stay behind in the City."

"And I told you the child will be no problem. I'll stay with my sister for a little while, and next season I'll join you again."

"What will I do in the meantime?" The man grabbed his crotch. "Already now you deny me your body."

The woman kept still looking at Viran. "I heard you ask about the trail-master. He is in the large tent over there. You'll know him when you see him."

When Viran and the women walked away, the man called after them, "Think about my offer."

As the woman had said, he recognized the trail-master easily. Big and bulky, his swarthy face covered by a thick gray beard, he sat on a pile of cushions, a tall jug beside him. Wiping the back of his large hand across his mouth, he looked at Viran out of watery gray eyes. "You must be from the island to the north," he said with a deep, but raspy voice. "I've had dealings with your people before. Usually you don't venture this far inland. Either you are lost or very brave."

Viran grinned. "I'm lost. I know if I walk west I would eventually come to the ocean, but I don't know how far south or north I've come."

"You are a three-day walk away from the bay where your people come on land, but it's also only three days from here to the City." The big man took a swig from his jug. "I am Oron," he said "What shall I call you?"

"I am Viran and these are my companions Mirtin and Vienne."

Oron grinned. "Your companions, hmm…? Why do they wear their hair so short?"

Viran shrugged, shook his own thick mane. "They come from a place far away. They have strange customs there."

"But they're women, aren't they?" The big man peered at Vienne. "I don't see any breasts."

"Oh, she's got them. Maybe she'll show them to you." Viran grinned.

Vienne hissed loudly beside Viran.

Oron laughed. "She has fire, I can see that." He waved his hand. "I'm an old man. In my younger days I might have taken a look, but now…" He sighed, scratched his balding head. "You're welcome to stay with us the night. Tomorrow we move on, you can decide then what you want to do."

"Thank you, Trail-Master," Viran said, bowed. "Maybe I can be of service to you."

"Not you, but maybe the Blond, the breast-less one." Oron laughed merrily. "Perhaps she can warm my old bones tonight."

Viran pushed Vienne out of the tent before she could open her mouth. She shook off his hand. "How dare you, you uncouth barbarian! I am not your woman."

"You are now, unless you want to fight off every male in this caravan." Viran told her. "I already made one mistake when I said that I was your guide."

"It is the truth."

"Not anymore. I claim you both as my women, and for your own sake you say it is so." Viran whispered fiercely. "That was Oron. He doesn't know me, but I have heard of him. Don't be fooled by his easy, friendly manners. He is a slave-trader. Look around you, there are no women here, except for the one you already met. There might be one or two more in the other tents. This caravan is on its way to the City to get more slaves, most of them will be females. These men will use them until they are sold."

"That is horrible. I can't believe that."

"It doesn't matter what you believe. I speak the truth." Viran gripped his war-hammer tightly, put the other arm around Mirtin and pulled her close. "Kiss me," he said with a low voice. "We are being watched."

Mirtin didn't hesitate. She put a hand behind his head, brought his face close to hers and kissed him passionately. Viran grinned when they broke apart. "I think that should convince them," he said quietly, and then with a loud voice. "Now, let us find something to eat."

He steered the women toward a group of men, who sat around a big fire, watching the carcass of a large animal being roasted.

"Safe journey." He used the formal greeting of the travelers, and then he told the women to sit down a short distance from him. When Vienne glared at him, he whispered, "Only men are allowed in the fire-circle. Do as I say!"

Mirtin pulled on Vienne's arm. Viran turned back to the watching men. He looked for an empty spot in the semi-circle the men had formed around the fire, found one and sat down. He put his war-hammer beside him, within easy reach. "I am Viran," he said. "Oron has given me permission to stay."

"We saw," one of them said.

"You seem to have a quarrel with your women. Do you not treat them right?" another one asked.

"We have not been together for long," Viran answered, carefully choosing his words. "They are unfamiliar with our ways. They need to adjust."

"Maybe we should take them off your hands," laughed the one beside Viran. The others joined his laughter.

"I might just take you up on that offer, sometimes I think they are more trouble than they are worth." Viran laughed loudly and made himself comfortable. He studied the men, counted eight. Usually there were around twenty men in a caravan, plus the women, if there were any. When he scanned the area he saw a few more men, busy with their wagons and animals. Most of the men sprouted beards. A sure sign that they were True-Humans. For some reason, which Viran didn't know, the Xandra-born males didn't grow facial hair.

Viran rubbed his hand across his own stubble. Among his people most men preferred to keep their faces free of hair, as did Viran. Only on gathering missions and hunting trips did the men grow beards.

One of the men pushed a knife into the roasting carcass, watched the juice run down the rusty blade. "I think it is done," he announced. With the help of another one he lifted the blackened, steaming body off the fire and laid it onto a large mat. Then he began cutting off large chunks of meat, which he speared with short sticks. These he handed to the watching men.

Viran accepted the one they offered him and asked for another piece for the women. Taking it, he got up and walked over to Mirtin and Vienne. "Be careful," he whispered. "I don't trust these people." Then he went back to join the men. The meat tasted gamy and was only partially done, but Viran ate it with gusto. He washed it down with sour wine from a flask they passed around.

When the flask was empty, someone produced another one, and soon the men were quite drunk, including Viran.

The sun had disappeared behind the mountains and darkness fell swiftly.

"I think I better join my women," Viran said with a thick tongue and rose to his feet.

"You can use my tent. I'll sleep in my wagon," one of the men offered and grinned. "Unless you want to share your women with me."

They all laughed drunkenly.

"Where is your tent?" Viran asked, squinted at the man. When he saw double images he rubbed his eyes. "I can't seem to see very clearly."

"I'll take you to it," the man said.

"Good." Viran stood for a moment, swaying, then stumbled over to where the women sat. Sinking to his knees, he grinned at Vienne. "I come to claim you for the night," he said loudly. "My friend has offered me his tent."

"You are drunk," Vienne said, disgustedly."

"Too much wine," Viran agreed.

"Come," said the man, who had followed Viran. He led Viran and the women to one of the tents. Before Viran crawled inside the man handed him a small flask. "Here," he said, "have some more wine, for you and your women." He laughed. "Call me if you need help."

Vienne ripped the leather flask out of Viran's hand. "I'm thirsty," she said, "besides, the meat tasted awful. I need to wash that taste out of my mouth." She took a long swig. Making a face, she put the flask down. "What is this? Does anything taste good in this place?"

Viran took it from her, put it to his lips. "They are not famous for their wine," he said, belched loudly and offered it to Mirtin. She drank some of it, but handed it back to him. "Vienne is right. This is awful stuff."

Viran laughed and drank most of the remaining wine. He dropped onto the fur-covered floor and fell into a deep, drunken stupor.

When he awoke, his head seemed ready to explode into a million tiny pieces, and when he tried to move, he found he couldn't. His hands were tied behind his back and his feet were wrapped tightly together with strong ropes.

Chapter Thirteen

Commander Beringer's face was cold with anger when he looked at the old man who called himself *The Sniffer*. "You are just as responsible for their deaths as are the men who murdered them," he said. They had found eight dead males and two, who were wounded, but still alive.

None of the females had been injured.

"I told you, I am also a victim. I've never killed anyone." The old man rung his hands, his blue eyes glistened with moisture.

"Words can kill as easily as any weapon." Beringer turned away, disgusted. He walked back to the group of women. They had dressed themselves again in their gray robes, which had been ripped off their bodies by the bounty-hunters.

The young woman, who spoke to him before, saw him approach. She smiled at him, shyly. He couldn't help but notice her extreme beauty. Her dark long lashes made her large bright-green eyes seem almost colorless. Her full lips had a natural red color and, even though the shapeless robe she wore now hid her body, he remembered the fullness of her naked breasts.

She shook back her long black hair, came up to him and looked into his eyes.

"Thank you," she said and kissed him on the lips.

Beringer felt slightly embarrassed by her show of affection. He glanced over to Starmote, who busied herself hobbling the horses so they couldn't run away. "I only did what any descent human being would have done," he said with a somewhat disturbed feeling. When he looked at this young woman he felt an attraction similar to what he felt with Starmote.

"I am Reyna," she said. "We were on our way to the harvest festival in the City. Maybe you want to accompany us there? I would be happy to join with you to collect your seed for the Great Mother."

"I don't quite understand," Beringer said.

"She wants to copulate with you," Starmote said behind him.

"It would be an honor," Reyna said brightly.

The Commander lifted both his hands in a defensive gesture, momentarily lost for words.

Reyna opened her robe and let it slip to the ground. Naked, she looked up at Beringer. "Don't you find me desirable?" she asked.

He stared at her breasts, at the small, black triangle below her flat, smooth belly.

"I am without a seed-pouch," Reyna said, "but I will give myself to you right now, if you want to. I owe you that much."

"You don't owe me a thing." Beringer found it difficult formulating the words. The pounding in his loins proved almost overpowering. *This is crazy*, he thought, taking a deep breath. He became aware of a pungent, strong, sweet odor in the air. Without thinking he pulled the filter mask over his nose. He looked for Wang and found him talking to a couple of the women. As he watched he saw one of them expose her breasts.

"Lieutenant Wang!" he bellowed. "On the double!"

Wang turned, came running. "Yes, Commander. Sir!"

Beringer noticed his flushed face. He grabbed the young lieutenant's arm, took him aside. "Do you feel sexually aroused?" he asked in a low voice.

Wang stared at him. "Beg your pardon, sir, I don't understand the question."

"Relax, Wang, this is private, just between two men. Do you feel horny?"

"I do, sir, but I have it under control."

"Just as I thought. It must be in the air. Wear your filter at all times."

The lieutenant pushed up his filter, took a few deep breaths. "I am fine, sir," he said. "With your permission, I'll tend to the wounded."

"Go ahead, Lieutenant."

Beringer walked back to Reyna. Still naked, she watched him with those green eyes. Starmote, who stood beside her, gave him an apprehensive look. "I'm sorry," he said. "I mean no offence. You are very beautiful, but forgive me, I am unfamiliar with your customs. Where I come from, we don't...ah...join with everyone we meet." He smiled. "Not immediately, anyway. So, please, put your clothes back on. I'm not used to having beautiful young ladies strip in front of me."

His eyes rested on Starmote. "Not that I mind, of course," he chuckled, trying to make light of the situation and felt like a complete fool when he saw Starmote smirk. "It's the air," he said to her, "there is something in the air."

"It's a pheromone, Commander. I've analyzed it. It comes from those plants by the shore," Starmote said.

Beringer saw the purple flowers that covered the shore line of the creek. "They're beautiful," he said.

"And dangerous."

"Dangerous? How?"

"They are carnivorous. I've watched one devour a small flying reptile that landed on it, but don't worry, they are too small to be of any concern."

"What about the scent they exude? I consider that dangerous."

Reyna, who had listened to their conversation, laughed. "There is no danger. We call it the *Flower of Love.* It smells much stronger at night, and it makes men go crazy."

"An aphrodisiac," Starmote said and smirked again. "You better keep those filters over your nose, Commander."

"I intend to do just that," he said stiffly. Turning back to Reyna, he asked, "Why do those bounty hunters kill only your men?"

Reyna shrugged. "They would have joined with us, against our will, and then, after they tired of us, we would have been sold as slaves."

Beringer cursed loudly. "I am glad we killed those bastards!" He looked at Starmote. "We've named this planet *Nu-Eden.* We Humans have always searched for our lost paradise. We thought we had found such a place. Maybe if we would have tried to get along with the local life forms, this could indeed have turned out to be a paradise. Looks like we're getting along alright."

"The Genaar do not condone slavery. They believe that every being has the right to be free." Starmote's face showed no expression. "Of course, reality is not always ideal. Some of us have no choice in what we are, no one is completely free."

"You are not free?" Beringer asked.

Starmote smiled. "I am as free as is possible for someone like me. My choices are limited. I am happy with what I am, because I was designed that way. But you, Commander, you don't seem happy with the choices you've made."

"My choices were always clear to me. My father was a soldier, and before him, his father." Beringer gave Starmote a thoughtful look. "Some day you'll have to explain to me the term *designed.* I am curious."

"Some day, maybe, I will. Some day I may tell you about the Genaar and their gentle ways, Commander. They have a long history.

You may be surprised at what you learn. Don't be too harsh on your own kind." Starmote turned and strode away.

Beringer watched her walk up to one of the horses and pat the animal's muscular neck. The horse snorted, nuzzled its long head against her shoulder.

A hand plucked gently on Beringer's sleeve. He looked into Reyna's bright green eyes. "You seem angry and sad," she said, smiling gently, "I can make you happy." She shrugged. "Or if you don't want me, any one of my sisters would be willing. All of us, if you like."

Against his will Beringer had to laugh. "You are certainly quite persistent, Reyna. Are you saying that you are all sisters?"

"We were all born of the Xandra. We have one mother. We are her daughters."

"I never thought of it that way. I guess that makes you sisters alright." Beringer took her hand into his. "Just so you know, I am flattered by your offer. You are such a lovely young girl, and so are all of your sisters, you are all beautiful. But no offence, I cannot accept your offer. We will accompany you to the City, if you like. You can show us the way."

Reyna clapped her hands together and laughed. "That is wonderful. We will be safe with you." She lifted up on her toes and kissed him on the cheek. Then she ran toward the creek to join her sisters, who had shed their robes and were swimming naked in the water.

Children, he thought to himself. *They are nothing but children in grown-up bodies.*

Reyna stood naked for a moment. The bright sun bathed her slim body with a golden light. She turned around, saw him watching her. She smiled, waved and dove gracefully into the water.

Beringer sighed and walked slowly to where Lt. Wang finished up with the two wounded men. Wang looked up when he heard his commander approach. "They'll live," he told him. "Both of them have only flesh wounds. One was shot in the shoulder, the other one in the leg."

Beringer nodded to the two wounded men. "I am Les Beringer," he said. "I am sorry we couldn't be here sooner, we might have been able to save the others, too."

The man with the bandaged shoulder smiled and held out a hand. "I am Vic. My brother's name is Torka. We are both grateful." He squinted at the commander. "You are *woman-born*, why are you helping us? Those men you killed were your own kind."

Beringer shook his head. "They were not my kind. They were murderers, criminals. They got what they deserved."

Vic studied him out of dark eyes. He had a smooth face, without even any stubble. Beringer found it difficult to determine his age. "There are True-Humans in the City who talk like you. They worship the Xandra, our mother, but you are a stranger. I can tell by your clothing." His gray eyes went to Starmote. "The woman with you, she is different. She looks like a water-nymph, but she is not."

"We come from far away, and we come in peace." Beringer said.

"Then come with us to the City, celebrate the harvest-festival with us."

Beringer chuckled. "Reyna invited us already and I told her that we would be happy to accompany you."

Torka laughed happily. "Reyna is very skilled in the ceremonial seed-taking. She will give you much pleasure."

"I'm sure she would," Beringer said, "but there is someone else whom I desire."

Both, Vic and Torka, noticed the flicker of his eyes toward Starmote.

"You are betrothed? I understand. A human custom." Vic said.

"Oh, no." Beringer lifted a hand. "I don't even know if she likes me."

"True-Humans are strange." Torka said. "We of the Xandra-born don't have those problems." He looked at Lt. Wang. "How about you? Will you join with one of my sisters?"

Wang seemed embarrassed, but he kept his face passive. "If my duties allow it, I may," he said, somewhat stiffly. He adjusted his nose-filter and took a deep breath. "I think we should bury the dead. Do you have any tools we could use to dig some graves?"

Vic waved him off. "There is no need. Tonight the scavengers will come and clean up."

"We can't just leave the bodies lying around," Wang protested. "They deserve a descent burial, even if those men were criminals."

"We have no tools for digging." Torka explained. "Even if we did, we couldn't bury the dead deep enough. The scavengers would just dig them up again, and they would be angry with us. It is the way."

"Talk about strange customs," muttered Wang.

"Where do you people come from?" Beringer asked Vic.

Vic pointed toward the direction the sun was heading for. "We live in a valley about five days from here."

"Forgive my inquiries, but I am interested. I don't know much about the way of life in your world. What do your people do where you live?"

Vic shrugged. "We live. We gather berries. We pick fruit from trees that we cultivate. The women weave baskets and blankets. They make pottery, but mostly we celebrate being alive." He grinned and snapped his hips back and forth.

Beringer remembered one of the entries in Captain Cunningham's journal: *We copulate all the time.* "Is that what the Xandra tells you to do?" he asked.

"The Great Mother tells us to love each other." Vic replied. "What else is there?"

"Don't you ever plant seeds or built things?"

"Why? The Mother makes everything grow. Only True-Humans waste time planting and building."

"I notice that you have a wagon to transport your belongings. Who built that?"

"We trade. Our crafts are popular with the people in the City. But enough now with all these questions, my head is beginning to hurt. I will go bath with the women."

Beringer watched Vic and Torka run to the river. Before they reached the shore they were already naked.

"They have no technology, they don't build, they travel on foot. I bet, none of them can read or write, and yet--they are happy." He looked at Wang. "I am curious to see how the people in the City live. From what I gather, the True-Humans live in harmony with the Xandra-born. If there is any danger on this planet, I don't believe it comes from the Xandra."

"What shall we do with the old man?" Wang asked.

"The Sniffer?" Beringer shrugged. "Give him a horse and tell him to get the hell away from here."

"Do you think it's wise?"

"Probably not, he deserves killing, but I am not a cold blooded murder."

When Beringer heard the soft drumming of the horse's hooves on the grass covered ground he didn't even turn around to watch the old man ride away. His eyes were on Starmote, who stood in the water. She had removed her clothing and rubbed her hands over her body. Seeing her like that, a sudden desire threatened to overwhelm him. He had guessed that she had a beautiful body, but naked she looked even more beautiful than he imagined. Her breasts were solid and firm, like two perfect halves of a globe. Even without the tight fitting clothing her waist stayed narrow. The sun's rays reflected in the sheets of water which she splashed over her body. It made her golden skin glow with a soft fire.

She submerged herself in the water, only her head rose above the surface. When she turned her head, she saw him watching her. She smiled, disappeared completely. Appearing again, she rose and walked slowly toward shore, climbed onto dry land.

She stood, watching him out of her large, dark eyes her short hair plastered to her head like a tight skull cap.

Beringer seemed frozen, unable to move. His eyes were glued to the small, black triangle below her flat belly. *She has no navel*, he thought. *She is totally alien.*

"I wish I had a towel," she said, loud enough for him to hear, and bent to pick up her clothing.

Her voice broke the spell that held him and he became acutely aware of his rapid heartbeat and an almost painful erection. He cursed her silently when she walked toward him, naked, carrying her clothing in one hand and her boots in the other. He couldn't help but admire her extremely long legs.

"Why don't you take a dip?" she asked, standing in front of him. "The water is refreshing."

He stared into her black eyes, fought the urge to throw her into the soft grass and thrust his erect penis into her smooth belly.

Only vaguely did his mind register the specks of golden color embedded in her white skin. Most of her body, except for her face, seemed covered with a faint, delicate pattern, like a tattoo, but he recognized it as a natural part of her skin.

"Maybe later," he said. His voice sounded like rough gravel. "I think I'll help Lt. Wang move the dead bodies away from the camp. We'll stay with these people tonight."

Stiffly, he turned and walked away. He heard her soft laughter, and again he cursed her for being so beautiful and seductive.

Chapter Fourteen

Viran watched helplessly as the men violated Mirtin and Vienne. They had tied the women to stakes driven into the ground, their arms and legs spread apart.

The man, who had so graciously offered Viran his tent for the night, grinned at Viran as he threw open his robe. He fondled himself to an erection and dropped between Vienne's spread thighs. She struggled in vain to free herself from her bonds. With one forceful thrust the man entered her. When she screamed in pain and frustration, he put his mouth over hers, cursed when she bit him. He backhanded her across the mouth, began to snap his hips back and forth.

Mirtin just lay there. Her eyes stared into the face of the man who labored above her. "I will kill you, if I ever get the chance," she said softly.

The man laughed, his buttocks quivered and he lay still while he erupted inside her. Mirtin closed her eyes when another man took his place.

As hard as Viran might try, he couldn't break his bonds.

Vienne gave up her struggles. She lay unmoving, her blue eyes large and unseeing. One of the others, who were watching, stepped closer. His robe stood open, exposing his erection. "Hurry it, Bronn," he said hoarsely. "Don't claim her for yourself."

Viran recognized him as the one they had talked to when they first entered the camp.

"It's been a long time since I had a real woman," Bronn growled. "I want to enjoy this one."

"So do I, come finish up," cursed the other one. "I'm almost ready to spill it."

"Then spill it. Use her mouth, it's big enough."

"She has sharp teeth." The man grabbed Bronn's long hair, pulled him backwards. Bronn cursed, pulled out of Vienne, his penis spurted his seed uselessly into the grass. He struggled in the other man's grip, tried to push his organ back into Vienne, but he finished before he could succeed.

His companion laughed, shouldered him aside and fell between Vienne's thighs. But before he could enter her Bronn appeared behind him, brandishing a long blade. With a loud curse he pushed it into the other one's back, right between the shoulder blades. Giving the knife a vicious twist, Bronn pulled it out again.

Without a sound, his companion collapsed on top of Vienne, a circle of red appeared on his robe as the blood spilled out of him. His body convulsed one more time, and then he lay still.

"Bronn killed Tremneck!" shouted one of the watchers.

Viran saw Oron, the trail-master, stride up to the group. "By the many faces of the Xandra," he cursed when he saw the lifeless body of Tremneck on top of Vienne. Glaring at Bronn, he bellowed, "Did you have to kill him over a woman?"

"He mocked me one too many times," Bronn defended his action.

"If I didn't need you I'd leave you for the night-creatures," Oron said. "Get rid of Tremneck's body, all his possessions belong to me, including his woman. Now, untie these women. I don't want any of you touching them again. They are much too valuable."

"What about the barbarian?"

"Just watch him, and take no chances with him. He'll fetch a good price." Oron stalked away.

Viran looked after him, cursed himself for being so stupid. The wine they had given him and the women had obviously been poisoned. A painful cramp in his belly sent waves of nausea throughout his body, and he felt drained of his strength.

The grass he lay on cooled during the night, but the rising sun already burned down on his bare upper torso. Even though the sun had bronzed his skin, lying exposed in the heat would soon dehydrate him.

He watched as a couple of the men untied Mirtin and Vienne. "Can I have my clothes back?" Vienne asked.

"And deprive us of looking at your beautiful naked body?" one of them said with a leer on his face.

"A shame I didn't get to sample it," the other one said, "but there still might be a chance." He elbowed his companion in the chest. "Eh, Togran, I don't think Aralda will be too pleased when she hears the good news that she belongs to Oron now."

They laughed again. "She might just slip a knife between his ribs when he sleeps."

"Can you at least untie my hands, please," Mirtin said. "Where would I run to?"

Togran shrugged his shoulders. "You're right, where indeed. Your protector is bound and helpless." He cut both women's ropes. Vienne rubbed her wrists, looked at Mirtin, who shook her head.

Viran had hoped that they might try to break free, but realized that without their strange lightning-throwers they were as helpless as he.

Vienne walked up to Viran, looked down at him. "Fine protector you turned out to be. And a great guide. You led us right into this predicament. If you weren't bound yourself I would think you were part of this group of extraordinary men." She grimaced and looked at Mirtin. "Those huge muscles are just show, that's all."

Mirtin smiled ruefully, started to bend down, when Togran stopped her. "Stay away from him or I'll tie you up again. Now, go down to the lake and take a bath."

"Can I have something to drink?" Viran called after Togran.

"Lick the dew off the grass," Togran said and laughed.

Viran turned onto his belly, tried to worm his way toward the lake. If he made it to the water, perhaps he could submerge himself and swim toward safety. He had the ability to hold his breath for a long time. Sharp blades of grass cut his face and skin as he pushed himself forward. He almost made it, when a heavy foot pinned him against the ground.

"Where do you think you're going?"

Viran twisted his neck, gave Oron a crooked smile. "I'm thirsty," he said. His voice sounded raw from lack of moisture, he didn't have to pretend.

"I'll have Aralda bring you some water," the trail-master said and spat onto the ground. "I am not an unreasonable man. After all, your health is important to me. You're no good to me sick, or even dead." He rolled Viran onto his side. "You better stay here or I may change my mind about your health." He grinned down at Viran. "I have nothing against you. You seem to be a likable man. But I am a trader, a businessman, and you are a profitable commodity, that's all."

"You have no honor," Viran said.

Oron laughed, spat again and wiped his big hand on his beard. "Honor is for stupid men, it buys you nothing." He stalked away.

It wasn't long before Viran heard someone approaching. The woman Aralda. She carried a small flask made from clay. She squatted beside him and put the flask to his lips. Viran gulped down the warm and tepid water, to his dry throat it tasted like the finest wine.

"Thank you," he said after quenching his thirst.

"I'll get some water from the lake to wash you off." She got up and walked down to the lake. When she knelt beside him again, she poured the water over his chest and rubbed him down with her hands.

"You have big muscles," she said, her hand lingering on his biceps.

Viran grinned. "Much good they've done me."

Aralda bent closer to his ear. "I can help you get away," she whispered.

"Why would you do that?"

She spat into the grass. "Oron has claimed me for himself. He will use me until he is tired of me, then he will sell me into slavery. As you know, I am with child, it is Tremneck's. Oron will kill my child as soon as it is born, maybe even while it is still in my belly. There is no room for children in a trade-caravan." She looked at Viran with a calculating expression. "If I help you to escape, will you take me with you?"

"I have no need for a woman who carries a child," Viran said.

Aralda opened the front of her robe and let him look at her breasts. They were nicely shaped, round and full. "Even though I have a child in my belly, I can still give a man pleasure. See." She opened her robe wider to let him see her stomach. "My belly is only swollen a little. I have a firm body and my *nest* is soft and moist."

"I'll take you with me," Viran said, staring at the thick black triangle below her round belly, "but I cannot keep you."

"Just take me to the City. I have a sister there." She let him look a little longer, then she closed her robe. She finished washing him off, got up and left.

Viran tried to make himself as comfortable as possible. Watching the camp, he counted altogether twenty-two men and seven women, including Aralda. They were getting ready to leave the next morning. Every man had his own horse. The women rode in one of the wagons, basically rectangular boxes with wheels. The wagons were covered with large leather sheets tied to bent wooden poles.

When evening came one of the women brought Viran a badly charred piece of meat on a stick and a flask filled with wine. Viran sat up, looked at the young woman. She could have been pretty, had it not been for the sullen look on her face. Her hair hung tangled and unkempt past her shoulders.

"Untie my hands so I can eat," he said, staring at her deep cleavage. *At least she's got nice breasts*, he thought.

She saw him looking, and pulled her robe closer around her with one hand, with the other she held the flask against his dry lips. "I'm not stupid," she hissed. When she spoke he saw the large gap where some of her teeth were missing.

"I didn't mean to imply that," he said, smiled. "I'm not used to being handfed by a beautiful young woman. A man should feed himself."

"I'm not beautiful," she said, averting her eyes. "I was told to feed you, that's all. So, please, eat."

"Will you be punished if I don't eat?" he asked.

"Don't ask questions. Just eat."

The meat turned out to be tough and dry, hard to chew. She watched him swallow it and gave him something to drink. "I hope this wine is not poisoned," he grimaced when the sour liquid ran down his parched throat. "Somehow it tasted better last night."

She almost smiled. "I saw you talking to Aralda," she said with a low voice. "Don't trust her. She is Oron's woman now." She rose and walked away swiftly.

It was getting darker and colder. Viran listened to a group of men who were gathering around a fire. Not close enough to hear every word, but from what he heard, it became clear that they intended to raid a small settlement of Xandra-born the next day. The men would be sold to work in the salt-mines, and the females taken north to be sold as concubines and sex-slaves.

Viran had never been in the north-country. A man who called himself the *Sergeant* ruled it with a ruthless hand. Viran didn't know much about the people who lived there. Even Orin, the Teacher, who knew a lot about the history of the world, had known very little. Apparently, when the first Humans appeared on the Xandra-world, the Great Mother ate many men and women. Some fled to the north, where the Xandra-plant could not exist.

One such fugitive, a great warrior named *The Sergeant*, took his soldiers and a group of women and began to populate the north-country. Over time they moved farther south, expanding their empire. They had found the secret of resisting the Xandra's call and eradicated all Xandra-plants.

The title *Sergeant* was handed down from one ruler to the next, usually a son or another warrior who proved himself ruthless enough to take control.

The Sergeant's people hated all Xandra-born and would never except them as equals. Either they killed them or used them as slaves. Viran's people, who lived on an island, away from the Great Mother's influence, did not hate the Xandra-born Humans. They respected the

Mother of Light, acknowledged the right to live for all her creatures, even the Neanders and the Zombs.

They were all part of *The World*.

Viran's people did not condone violence, especially not murder, but they accepted it as a way of life.

However, these people were evil in Viran's eyes. He would stop them, given the chance. He watched as the fire burned down. Most of the men crawled into their tents. Only one guard stayed by the fire. The two *Wanderers* were hidden behind a low hanging bank of clouds, leaving the night in darkness. Viran's sharp ears heard the soft rustling sound in the grass as someone approached his position. Moments he saw Aralda walking up to him.

She crouched down beside him. "Hush," she whispered, "don't make any noise." She had a knife which she used to cut his bonds. Viran rubbed his wrists and ankles and stretched his cramped muscles.

"We'll need a couple of horses," Aralda said, "but we have to wait. Ortaka is standing guard. He'll be asleep in a short time." She stretched out beside Viran and slid on top of him. He felt her soft breasts warm against his bare chest. Her hand slid along his belly. With deft fingers she undid his belt, and then her fingers curled around his manhood.

"It's not just your muscles that are big," she whispered into his ear and giggled when his penis reacted to her squeezing.

"There is no need for this," Viran said.

"I have the need," Aralda said, pushed his breeches past his knees, moved down and sucked him into her mouth. Viran groaned as her tongue flicked over his swollen glans. When his erection became almost painful in her warm mouth he pulled her gently off him. "Let's not waste my seed in your mouth," he said and put her onto her back.

She laughed throatily. "I guess there is no chance you'll give me another child, since I carry one already inside my belly," she said and let him open her robe. Her thighs parted willingly, and with gentle force Viran sheathed his rigid organ in her hot flesh. She gasped, put a fist into her mouth to keep from crying out.

"Am I hurting you?" he asked.

"No," she murmured and began to move underneath him. "It's been a long time since a man entered me so gently. Tremneck hurt me most of time." She smiled. "I did not expect such gentleness from a barbarian."

Viran chuckled. "I do not consider myself a barbarian. My people are no less primitive than yours."

She didn't answer. Wrapping her long legs around his waist, she pushed up against him. It didn't take long before her floodgates opened and doused him with warm liquid. Enjoying her fiery passion, he held back as long as he could. When he felt the flames flare up inside him, he let their heat consume his body and mind and erupted with a suppressed grunt inside her flowing orifice. She raked his bare back with clawed fingers. He pressed his mouth on hers to keep her from screaming. When he wanted to pull out of her, she kept milking his still hard organ and strong legs clamped around his torso.

"Not yet," she sobbed, "not yet."

Unaware of his surroundings, Viran froze when a voice spoke harshly beside him. "Get off my property!" He had to pry Aralda's thighs open forcefully so he could slip out of her tight embrace. She opened her eyes, gasped and sat up, trying to pull her robe around her naked body.

"Don't bother covering up. I may just decide to let all the men use you!" Oron bellowed and kicked at Viran, still on his knees and hampered by his breeches, which he had pushed down to the tops of his boots.

"Very clever, Barbarian," Oron sneered. "You thought you could escape by coupling with my woman."

"She is not your woman," Viran growled.

"Are you claiming her then for yourself?" Oron tried to kick Viran again, but Viran rolled away, pulled up his breeches at the same time. He rose to his feet with a smooth movement, stood facing the trail-master. Only now he saw the woman behind the other man and identified her as the one who had brought him his food earlier that night. One of the Wanderers rose past the cloud, in its pale light Viran saw the woman's smug smile. The gap in her teeth made her look like an old hag.

"I told you she would try to free him," she said to Oron.

"Yes, you did," Oron rasped, "now go back to Vicandro and tell him to bring a couple of men to help me handle this savage!"

She put her hand on the trail-master's arm. "I hope you won't forget what I did," she cooed.

He waved her off. "Don't worry, you'll get what's coming to you. Now, go!" The pale light of the moon reflected in his eyes. They glinted with a cold fire beneath his thick eyebrows. "You," he said to Aralda, "I'll deal with you later. Go and wait for me in my wagon."

Aralda lowered her eyes, wrapped her robe tightly around her body and without looking back she hurried away.

Oron glared at Viran. "You know, I hoped to make a profit with you, but I think I will take a loss. You are trouble. Who knows, next time you might succeed, and I can't allow that." He carried what looked like a long stick in his hands, but Viran knew what it was. Oron pointed it at him.

Viran saw the bright flame, heard the sharp crack. A heavy weight smashed into his chest, threw him backwards. His feet gave away underneath him. Finding himself lying on the ground, it surprised him that he didn't feel any pain. He felt nothing at all. When he tried to move he couldn't. Strange, his thoughts were surprisingly clear. He saw Oron bending over him and poking him with the fire-stick.

"Is he dead?" asked a woman's voice. He recognized the young woman with the missing teeth. There were three men with her. One of them carried Viran's war-hammer.

"Go, get Aralda," Oron told the young woman. Moments later Aralda stood beside Oron. She looked down at Viran, the horror evidenced in her eyes.

"All that blood," she gasped. "You killed him. Why?"

"He is not dead," Oron said, "the spark of life is still in his eyes." He took Viran's big hammer, handed it to Aralda. "Here, you put him out of his misery."

She took a step backwards, put her hands over her mouth. "No," she stammered, "don't make me do that."

Oron grabbed her by her hair, pulled her close. "You do as I say or I'll put a bullet into your head, right now!" He forced the war-hammer into her hands. "Do it!"

She stood there, holding the big hammer awkwardly. Her eyes were large. Viran saw with strange clarity the tears rolling down her cheeks.

Do it!" Oron thundered.

She screamed, lifted the heavy weapon over her head.

The second moon had risen. The big hammer-head glowed dully in the eerie bright light of the two Wanderers as it descended in slow motion. It blotted out part of the night-sky. Then it smashed into Viran's face. Darkness came swiftly.

Chapter Fifteen

"They are half-human, half-animal," Beringer said to Starmote. They lay in darkness, watching the scavengers go about their grisly business. He magnified the image in his small pocket scope, zoomed in on one of the creatures.

Dripping saliva, it sank its long fangs into the corpse it held in its clawed hands, ripped out a large piece of bloody flesh. It roared in defiance and rose on its powerful short hind legs when another of the creatures tried to share the bounty. Flashing gleaming teeth and sharp claws, they lunged at each other. A third one dragged the carcass the two were fighting over into nearby shrubs and began to rip it apart.

Some of the creatures walked erect, like men. When they went down to move on all fours, their shoulders were higher than their buttocks, because of their extremely long arms.

Even through the long shaggy hair, which covered their bodies, Beringer noticed that some of them had human looking breasts. Those were obviously the females. He wondered about that. According to Captain Cunningham's journal, the creatures, which the Xandra created, were not fertile. Why then would she create males and females? He didn't see any tails.

"What a way to dispose of your dead companions," Starmote said and took off her distance-goggles. "I'm going to get some sleep. You better come, too, Commander. It has been a long day."

"Are you inviting me?" he asked, grinning.

She smiled. "Just because every female in this camp asks you to join with her, doesn't mean I'm one of them. Sorry, Commander, you had your chance, but you decided not to accept my offer." She walked away, looked back over her shoulder. "Of course, there is always the chance I might change my mind. But not tonight."

Beringer looked after her. The light from the two satellites threw double shadows ahead of her, one shorter than the other. Even though she wore baggy clothing, he could see her full round buttocks moving under the thin, but tough material.

Sighing, he stood up and followed her slowly. As her superior, at least on this mission, it would not be smart to press the issue.

The fragrance from the purple flowers seemed much stronger now. Even his nose-filters could not completely mask it. It took all of his willpower to resist the temptation to sleep with one of the Xandra-females. Any one of them would welcome him.

Lt. Wang sat cross-legged in front of one the tents. He seemed to be sleeping, but when Beringer approached he opened his eyes. "It's a beautiful night," he said. "So peaceful."

"If you can ignore the howls of joy from the banquet table," Beringer said, squatting down beside his lieutenant.

They had carried the dead men to the edge of the valley, far away from the camp, but the growls and barks coming from the beastly scavengers carried far in the silence of the night.

"What happened to this planet, Commander?" Wang asked.

Beringer shrugged. "That's what we have to find out. This is my first time on the surface. They commissioned us to protect the colonists from space. We were never supposed to be down here. That job belonged to Sergeant Vick's. Captain Cunningham and I became good friends, and he kept me well informed about what took place on Nu-Eden. At first we thought there was no intelligent life on the planet, until we discovered the Xandra. We still don't know what exactly we're dealing with. Is it just a self-aware plant or is it more than that? You saw what it is capable of. You were there when we burnt that plant on the station."

"How can I forget," Wang said. "What exactly did we kill there? Who was that woman? Was she real?"

"She was real, but we didn't kill a human woman, only a creation of the Xandra."

"Like these people here?"

"More than that. She was a manifestation of the Xandra herself," Beringer said. "From what I read in the Captain's journal, the Xandra-plant has the ability to take on human or animal form. But that is not her only ability. She can read thoughts, can possibly influence people's minds, and who knows what else."

"What about these men and women? How are they born?"

"They're grown in seed-pouches."

"They are not human, then?"

Beringer shrugged again. "I can't determine that. They have human fathers, which makes them at least half-human."

"What are those scavengers?" Lt. Wang stared into the night. The howls and barks had not stopped.

"They are the Xandra's creations. Captain Cunningham wrote about them in his journals. They all existed in somebody's mind. They are the legacy of the people the Xandra absorbed a thousand years ago. That is a long time to experiment."

Beringer closed his eyes, remembered one particular entry. "I've seen Angels and Demons," he murmured, a cold shiver running down his spine. "Who knows what other creatures she has created." He looked up at the bright disks of the two satellites. Strange, how different they looked from the surface of the planet. They seemed mysterious, foreboding almost. When looking at them in space they were nothing but two huge rocky spheres with a dust-covered surface, full of craters and ravines.

A shadow fell upon him. He looked into the face of one of the girl. She smiled, and then looked at Wang. The young lieutenant rose to his feet. "Sorry, Commander," he said, with embarrassment, "I have a date with Tamsy. I hope it is not against regulations."

Beringer shook his head, looked at the swell of the girl's breasts under the silky robe and tried to still the throb in his loins. "Go right ahead, Wang," he said, "but don't wander too far away from camp."

He watched the two young people walk away. Wang had one arm around the girl's slim waist. Suddenly quite tired, Beringer crawled into the tent. There were soft mats on the floor. He stretched out and closed his eyes.

Uneasy dreams haunted his sleep. He awoke drenched in sweat. It seemed stifling hot inside the tent. He took off his clothing and lay naked on the mat.

A soft rustling sound made him open his eyes, to find a dark shadow blocking the open entrance to the tent. "Wang?" he asked, his mouth full of cotton, "is that you?"

The figure didn't answer. Beringer sat up, searched for his palm-light in the darkness.

"Don't be afraid," said a soft female voice. A hand reached down, touched his shoulder.

"Who are you?" he demanded to know, still unable to think clearly.

"I am Naomi," she said and knelt down in front of him. She seemed to wear some kind of cloak around her shoulders. When she pressed against him, he felt soft naked breasts touching his skin. She pushed him onto his back, straddled him as he stretched out his body. Soft warm fingers curled around his penis. He moaned when it moved in her hand.

"Relax," she whispered, lifted up, hovered for a moment, and then she sank into his lap.

The release of the desire, which had burned inside him for days, made him shout when her soft sheath slid over his erect organ. He didn't know this woman and he didn't care. The only thing that mattered where those hot and wet tight walls that kept him prisoner.

He grabbed her slim hips, pulled her deeper into his lap. Her cloak opened, moved gently behind her, like a pair of giant wings. He felt a soft breeze. The flap, which covered the entrance to the tent, fluttered open. Light from the two moons flooded the interior. The woman on top of him became clearly visible, and he looked into her delicately formed face, registered the coal black skin. Above full, sensuous lips her nostrils slightly flared and her dark eyes glinted with a reddish glow.

His eyes traveled down to her small, conical breasts. She smiled, displayed a pair of needle-thin fangs. Before the light disappeared, he realized that what he had thought to be a cloak was actually a pair of wings.

"I am a *Shadow-Angel,*" she said, as if reading his mind. "I mean you no harm." She began pumping her bottom furiously. He could not contain the built-up pressure any longer, cried out and, lunging upwards, he exploded inside her. She stretched out on top of him, her lips touched his neck. At the height of his climax he felt a sharp pain as she sank her fangs into his jugular. Momentary dizziness, and then he experienced waves of pleasure radiating from his neck, down to his belly.

His orgasm subsided, but she did not release him, her muscles tightened around his still erect shaft. The inside of her vagina began to vibrate with a steady rhythm.

His whole body seemed aflame, her lips hot against his neck. "Don't worry, I won't drain you," she whispered into his ear. "I need very little."

She milked him with gentle pressure, brought him to another climax, and then another, all the while drinking his blood.

After the third climax he began to feel strangely lightheaded and tried to push her off. She laughed, pinning him down. For a slight girl she demonstrated exceptional strength.

"You said *only a little,*" he croaked.

She let go of him and lifted up. When his penis slid out of her he felt the need to enter her again. Holding her hips, he pushed up. She laughed, took him back inside her. Her eyes glowed red in the semi-darkness. "Your need is greater than mine," she said. "Here is my gift to you."

She began go gyrate her lower body, her alien vagina pulsed around his shaft, hot and wet. Again the burning flames of pure pleasure raced through his body, consumed his whole being. His thoughts became confused, his mind delirious. She rode him for a long time, her black wings flapping in the confines of the tent. When she finished with him, he felt exhausted and only half-conscious, his body drenched in sweat.

He never saw her leave.

The sound of voices brought him back to awareness. Sitting up, he looked around in the tent, noticed the blanket that lay crumpled in a corner. He shivered in the cold morning air.

He heard male voices. Strangers.

Dressing quickly, he reached for his gun, took off the safety. Then he stuck his head out of the tent. He saw horses, made a decision and stepped into view.

He counted six horses, only one of them had a rider. The other five men were talking to Lt. Wang and Starmote.

"Greetings," said the man on the horse. He looked young, like the others.

Beringer didn't see any hostility and holstered his weapon. "Greetings," he answered. "Who are you?"

The young man laughed. "We could ask you the same question. It is obvious that you are strangers to this part of the world."

"I am Beringer," the commander said, "You are correct, our home is far away from here."

"Are you going to the City?"

Beringer nodded. "We are. We promised to protect these people."

The young man looked at him thoughtfully. "They are *Xandra.* You are not."

"Neither are you, I assume," Beringer wasn't sure, took a guess.

"My brothers and I got the call. We will be taking part in the harvest-festival and the seeding celebration. This is my first time." The young man grinned and winked. "The first time in the City, that is. I've been with a *water-nymph*, so I'm not exactly ignorant."

"A *water-nymph*?"

Again the young man gave Beringer an odd look. "Yes, a water-nymph. Don't tell me you don't know about them."

Beringer shrugged. "I admit, I don't know."

"Where exactly are you from?"

"Across the ocean," Beringer said.

The young man nodded. "I've heard about the world that is supposed to exist on the other side of the ocean. My father knows more about it."

"He's been there?" Beringer asked, cursing his ignorance about this planet.

"Oh no, but as young man he met a group of men who claimed to be from a place where the Xandra did not exist. They told my father that they crossed the big water in a ship that sailed in the wind, but it crashed against the rocks and sank. Only a few of the men saved themselves. My father told many stories like that. Until now I never believed any of them. Did you come in a ship?"

Furiously thinking, Beringer nodded. "Yes, in a ship."

Before the young man could ask any more questions the arrival of a team of horses that appeared at the edge of the forest interrupted him. The horses were pulling a long covered wagon.

"There are my parents now," said the youth. "I'll talk to you later." He dug his heels into his horse's flanks, galloped away to meet his parents.

Beringer looked after him, wiping his forehead. Damn! He had to watch what he said. His mind felt a little fuzzy this morning. He remembered a winged girl. Had she been real or just a manifestation of this great sexual craving he felt building up inside him? Sniffing, he detected the strange fragrance still in the crisp air. When he looked at the river, he noticed that the purple flowers were only half-open.

"Good morning, Commander." He recognized Starmote's voice. She came walking toward him. "You look tired," she said. "Restless night?"

"Strange dreams plagued me last night," he said, not going into details. "This place is getting to me."

She laughed a little, stretched and yawned. Beringer stared at her breasts as they strained against the thin material of her shirt.

God, how I desire her, he thought and touched the side of his neck to scratch a sudden itch.

"You're bleeding," Starmote said.

He looked at the blood on his fingers.

Starmote put a hand on his cheek, made him turn his head. "Did you injure yourself?" she asked. "I see two puncture wounds on your neck. You scratched them open." She reached into her pocket, pulled out a small device and held it against his neck. "I detect minute amounts of venom. Were you bitten by some kind of reptile?"

"I don't remember."

He felt a sting as she touched his skin. "There," she said, "this should neutralize any alien substance, which might have entered your bloodstream."

"Who are these people?" he asked her.

"Farmers," she said.

"Friendly?"

She lifted her shoulders. "They do carry weapons, but I don't believe they're hostile. You've talked to one of them."

"A boy." Beringer chuckled. "You said they're farmers. Well, this boy seems eager to do some seeding."

"I don't know what you mean." Starmote looked at him. Her alien black eyes glinted in the morning sun.

I wonder if her lips are naturally red, he thought. Her shirt stood open around her neck. He saw the faint markings on her skin. *She's not human*. He tried to convince himself that he should not feel the way he did.

"Well, Commander?" she said, her face unreadable, even though she saw him stare at her partially exposed breasts. "Are you feeling alright? You seem distant."

"I'm fine," he said, wiping his brow. "They are on their way to the City, to perform some kind of fertility ceremony. It has something to do with the Xandra."

Beringer turned to watch the wagon pulling up beside them. Only now did he notice two more wagons behind the first one. He also saw the four huge hounds loping beside the wagons, big animals, with shaggy, brown coats. Beringer touched the butt of his gun in an instinctive motion. These animals could be dangerous, their huge jaws looked strong enough to tear out a man's throat with ease.

A man and a woman sat on a bench in the front of the first wagon. They were both elderly. The other two wagons carried one occupant each, young boys, younger than the one Beringer had spoken to.

The older man tied the reins that controlled the team of horses to a post on the side of the bench, and then he jumped off the wagon. He stretched his legs, looked at Beringer and touched his right hand to his upper left arm.

"Greeting," he said.

Guessing it might be some kind of a ritual when meeting strangers Beringer repeated the gesture. "Greeting," he said and smiled.

"My son tells me you are from the world that lies beyond these shores," the older man said. "A long time ago I met people who made the same claim."

"Sometimes our ships get lost," Beringer said.

The man took off his hat, gave it a few slaps with his other hand to shake out the dust. Beringer noticed his nearly bald head, the little bit of hair that framed part of his skull, gleamed gray white, just like his long, scraggly beard. Putting his hat back on his head, the old man peered at Beringer. "Did your ship get lost?" he asked.

The commander nodded. "In a way it did. We were heading north when we were blown off course. We crashed against some rocks, our ship sank. Only the three of us survived." The story seemed as good as any Beringer could come up with. He hoped the other man would not ask too many questions. "By the way, my name is Beringer," he said, "and this is Starmote."

"I am Esram," the older man said, studying Starmote. "She looks different, is she Xandra-born? She has the eyes of a water-nymph."

"She is different, but not Xandra-born. She is Starmote, that's all."

"Is she your mate?"

Beringer glanced at Starmote, smiled. "No," he said, "just a companion."

"Does she talk?"

"I talk when people look at me and into my eyes, even if they find them unattractive," Starmote said.

Esram laughed. "I don't find your eyes unattractive, just the opposite; as a matter of fact, it is not just your eyes that I find attractive."

"Don't mind him," said a voice from the wagon. The older woman. "He's trying to pretend he is still young and handsome." She climbed down from the wagon, walked toward them. Beringer noticed her slightly bulging belly under her long dress.

She saw his look, padded her stomach and smiled. "Even though he's old, he is still able to add to the numbers in our family." She stopped in front of Beringer, looked up at him. "I am Lyra, Esram's wife."

Years of bearing children and hard work had left their mark on her once pretty face, but her eyes were sparkling and full of life. *It is a pity*, Beringer thought. *On the ship or back on Earth her beauty could have been preserved, but here on this harsh planet her age is beginning to show.*

Lyra poked a finger at Starmote. "If I were you I wouldn't let a handsome man like this get away. Do you have any children?"

"Children?" Starmote was surprised at the question. "I don't have any children."

"No children! What a shame. When I was your age I had already two. Even my daughter, who just began her cycles, has already born a child of her own."

"That's very admirable," Starmote said cautiously, "but in my life there is no room for children."

Lyra waved her hand. "Don't say that. Children are very important. We try to have as many as possible. Mirna, my daughter, brought her son with her. That is the reason we are going to the City. Even though we are not Xandra-born we do worship the Great Mother. She will bless and mark the newborn child. All of my sons have been marked."

"Marked? I don't quite understand."

"Oh, that's right, you are strangers. Somehow I can't picture living without the Xandra in my life. Every male-child is required to be marked. When a boy becomes a man the Xandra knows this, and she calls him to her. Aran, my third youngest, it is his first time. He is a little wild sometimes, I know he's been with the water-nymphs already, can't say I blame him, his juices are probably overflowing. He'll fertilize many seed-pouches." She smiled proudly. "All my sons are very fertile."

Esram laughed beside her. "No wonder, look who's the father."

Lyra turned and planted a kiss on his nose. "How about some breakfast? I am starving."

"So am I. We've been on the road since before daybreak," he explained to Beringer and Starmote. "Would you care to join us?"

"I'll be happy to do so," Beringer said. "I haven't eaten since yesterday."

Chapter Sixteen

At first the Xandra-born were apprehensive of the newcomers, but after Lyra started talking with them, they joined the group at the small feast. Some of the girls, including Reyna, went to pick some fungus. They ate the white chunks raw, dipped into a sticky red liquid, which they carried in clay-jars.

Reyna offered some to Beringer. When he hesitated, she laughed and pushed it between his lips. "It is not harmful," she said, smiling. He chewed it and swallowed. The dip tasted like honey, and the fungus, except for being a little peppery, had almost no taste.

Lyra, who sat cross-legged beside Beringer, grabbed his knee and squeezed. "She likes you," she laughed, "don't eat too much of that stuff, unless you want to fill her little seed-holder. These Xandra-girls are natural seed-collectors, if you know my meaning."

The older woman's familiarity embarrassed Beringer a little. He looked at Esram, her husband, but he didn't seem to notice. His eyes were on Starmote.

Beside Esram sat the daughter, Mirna, so young, barely out of puberty, and already a mother. She smiled at Beringer when she saw him look at her. She had a somewhat coarse face. Her hair hung loose and wild around her shoulders. With a little makeup she could have been pretty.

"So, where is the father?" Beringer asked, his eyes glancing at the sleeping baby. Mirna sat cross-legged, like her mother, the short dress she wore bunched up, leaving her thighs bare. She saw his glance, blushed a little and pulled the rim of her dress a little higher, giving him a healthy view of her naked genital area.

Damn it! Beringer cursed silently. *Is this what all these people think of?*

"The father," Mirna said, "is back at the farm. Someone needs to keep an eye on things. I miss him already. I hope he misses me, too." She pouted. "With all those nymphs nearby, I doubt it, though."

Esram padded his daughter's hand. "Now, now, daughter. Don't be jealous. Rolard is a fine man, and he loves you." He looked at Beringer. "Rolard is my youngest brother. He took a fancy to Mirna ever since she was a little girl. And now that she is of age he made a woman out of her. The Xandra be thanked, she's not barren. It happens sometimes." Esram looked at Starmote. "Is that what the problem is with you?" he asked bluntly.

Starmote shrugged, took a sip of water from her canteen. "Who knows? I never had offspring. Probably never will, either."

"It takes two people to make a child, with Humans, that is." Lyra squeezed Beringer's thigh again, laughed throatily. "A good man could be of great help."

Starmote rose to her feet. "I'll go get the riding-animals," she said and stalked away.

Esram looked after her, took off his hat and wiped his bald head. "She's a strange one," he said. "Are you sure she's not *Xandra*?"

"I'm sure." Beringer glanced at Reyna, who sat on his other side, the only one of the Xandra-girls still eating. The others had gone to take down the tents. He wondered what kind of thought processes were going on inside her head. She looked human, but was she human? Inside she might be more alien than Starmote. Reyna saw his glance, smiled at him, ran her fingers gently down his arm.

"Those horses are fine looking animals," he heard Esram say.

"I wouldn't know," Beringer said absently. "First time I have seen live ones." Reyna's soft hand sent tendrils of delightful pleasure through his body. Images of a dark skinned winged girl appeared in his mind, a pulse in his groin began to throb. Lyra's hand on his thigh felt like a heavy weight. He shook his head to clear it and looked at Esram.

The older man didn't seem to notice Beringer's discomfort. He took a swig from a long-necked clay vessel and wiped his mouth. "Whose horses are they?" he asked and belched loudly.

"They belonged to the bounty-hunters," Reyna said. "Beringer and his friends killed them. He shoots lightning bolts from his hands." She stroked Beringer's arm. "He's a great warrior."

"I bet he is," Lyra laughed, her fingers digging into his flesh.

"So that's where those gnawed bones come from," Esram said. "I wondered about that." He rose, squinted at the sun. "I guess we'll get moving. I'd like to get to the Ballard-creek farm before nightfall. Let's hope we don't run into another group of those bounty-hunters. They don't care much for us Xandra-worshippers."

Lt. Wang helped the two remaining Xandra-men hitch a couple of horses to the wagon. The women already loaded the tents, and everything else they owned, into the wagon. Including the horses that belonged to the bounty-hunters, they now had eleven riding animals.

At first Beringer thought that most of the Xandra-born would ride in the wagon, but discovered the wagon packed full of supplies and trading goods. The wagons of Esram's group were filled to capacity with grain, leaving no room for hitchhikers

Reyna laughed when he brought up the subject of transportation. "We walk," she said. "We take turns riding the horses."

Starmote seemed a natural on the horse she had chosen. She swung herself on top of the big black stallion. The big animal reared up, but calmed down when Starmote padded the muscular neck.

Beringer felt awkward, foolish almost. He had some trouble even getting onto the back of the large animal. With no saddle, just a blanket, held down by straps pulled around the horse's belly, it proved quite difficult.

"Give me a hand here, Lieutenant," he called with a low voice. Wang laced his fingers together, let Beringer step onto the small platform. Sitting on the animal's broad back, Beringer watched Wang swing himself onto his horse.

"My father used to take me to a petting zoo when I was a kid," Wang explained to Beringer.

"It is obvious, you've never ridden before." Starmote pulled up beside him.

"I'm at home on a star-ship, not a horse." Beringer tried to keep his steed from bolting away. The horse sensed his uneasiness, lifted its head and blew air through its large nostrils.

Starmote laughed. "Relax, Commander, and don't pull so hard on the reins."

"I'm surprised to see you ride with such ease. They're wouldn't have been any horses where you come from."

"Not horses. But we had riding animals, huge and vicious scaly beasts who could take your head off with one bite. I grew up on a savage planet, Commander. I am used to handling violent creatures."

"Nothing surprises me anymore," Beringer said. "Some day you'll have to tell me more about your home world. Maybe it will help me to understand you better."

Starmote nodded. "I'm going to secure the rear, Commander," she said, "with your permission."

"Go ahead," Beringer said and thought *As if you care about my permission.*

Starmote clucked, turned her steed and galloped away.

The wagons were now moving with a steady pace, the creaking of the wooden wheels broke the silence of the morning. They were following a slightly overgrown dirt-road.

Beringer shifted the weight of his backpack and made himself more comfortable. His horse seemed to have accepted him. It walked stoically behind the last wagon. Another rider moved to Beringer's side. When he looked up, he recognized Aran, the young man he spoke to earlier.

"I've been listening to the Xandra-girls," Aran said. "They regard you as some kind of god. They all want to catch your seeds." He studied Beringer from the side. "You know, you are different, so is your friend Wang and that female with you. She is obviously not human. They say you slew six men in a matter of moments. They say that you threw lightning bolts at them. Is that true?"

Beringer smiled. "You are quite inquisitive, aren't you? We are not gods. I am as human as you are. It is true, we killed those men quite easily, but not with lightning bolts. We have superior guns, that's all."

"The one you carry on your hip, is that such a gun?"

Beringer nodded.

"It looks small," Aran said. "May I see it?"

"I'm sorry. I can't give it to you. It could kill you, if you don't know how to handle it."

"You could show me."

"I could and maybe I will, we'll see." Beringer smiled at Aran. He liked the young man. He seemed so eager, so hungry for knowledge. But he didn't know anything about Aran and his people and didn't see the need to become careless. "Tell me about your family and yourself. What do you do to survive?"

"We grow huit?"

"What is *huit*? What is it used for?"

"To make bread. It looks like tall grass with many seeds on top. We harvest the seeds. They are ground between large stones into flour. It has many other uses. My father makes a very strong wine from it."

"I understand. It must be very hard work."

Aran shrugged. "We use horses to pull the plows. When harvest time comes we get help from the *Xandra-Humans*; there is a large settlement not far from us. They are fairly good workers."

"How do you pay them?"

"Pay them?" Aran chuckled. "We let them live on our land, we let them pick fruit from our trees, we let them dig for clay so they can make their pottery. Xandra-Humans have no need for gold."

"You use gold to trade?"

"It is mostly used in the City. We get paid in gold when we deliver our *huit* to the City-traders. With the gold we can trade for other items that we need, like tools, cloths, and many other things." Aran hesitated. "You don't know that?" he asked, sounding surprised.

"I didn't. Where I come from we don't use gold as payment for goods and services. We have other means for compensation. Gold, to us, is just another metal, useful for many things, but so is silver or platinum."

"You have silver?" Aran asked excitedly. "It is very rare here, very valuable."

"Tell me about the bounty-hunters. Where do they come from?"

"Mostly from the east. It is not often they come this close to the City, but it is worse at the border. Not all Easterners are bounty-hunters, most just hate the Xandra-born. That is the reason the Xandra calls the human men to the City to collect seeds. The seedpods are not safe anymore on the ponds outside of the City."

"Who pays them for the killings?"

"*The Sergeant.*"

"Who is *The Sergeant*?"

Aran shrugged. "He is the leader of Numerika, the country to the north. Everybody knows that." He made a clucking sound with his tongue, galloped away toward the front of the wagon train.

Beringer looked after him, deep in thought.

The Sergeant. There had been only one sergeant on the planet's surface, Sergeant Vicks. Could it be...? He shook his head. Of course not! Vicks wouldn't be alive now, not after a thousand years. Somehow the name *Sergeant* had survived. Also, there existed a country named Numerika, headed by a man who called himself *The Sergeant*, and he hated the Xandra-born. Very interesting.

He looked forward to seeing the City. Maybe he would find some answers there.

He felt suddenly very tired. His eyes began to droop

...the dark, shapely body of the girl undulated above him. Her partially spread wings moved gently. Her hot vagina milked his engorged penis, made his blood race, his heart beat faster. His body

was aflame. He saw the gleaming incisors, felt the sharp pain in his neck...

His eyes flew open, he willed himself to stay awake. But his thoughts began to drift. He had time to reflect on the previous night's happening.

What exactly took place? He wasn't sure of anything. Had the winged girl been real? His fingers touched his neck where a pair of puncture marks seemed to tell a story. Maybe some kind of snake had bitten him, like Starmote suggested, and the venom had created hallucinations. The pheromones in the air, the open invitation of Reyna and her sisters, seeing Starmote naked, it was enough to drive any sane and healthy man to the edge.

Things had changed on the planet since the Humans tried to colonize it a thousand years ago. But what caused these changes? Here he was, riding a horse on a dusty dirt road, a method of transportation abandoned over a thousand years ago, (again he had to mentally correct himself: *Two* thousand years ago).

He turned to look at the group of girls who walked behind him. They seemed happy, singing along to music only they could hear. They had beautiful, clear voices. Looking at their lovely innocent faces and shapely bodies, Beringer wasn't really surprised. The Xandra loved perfection.

They walked barefoot. It didn't seem to bother them.

Starmote made up the rear. He could see her talking with the girls on horseback. She seemed to be comfortable with them.

They were beautiful people, harmless in their appearance. Were they? Could they be considered human? Beringer couldn't answer that question.

Sitting straight, he took a deep breath. The air smelled fresh, slightly scented. To his left the river gurgled as it wound itself through the changing land.

The road they traveled on followed the twisting turns of the river. Beringer noticed that the river became wider. The trees on the other side were scattered and the land changed into open prairie. Even on this side the forest began to thin, and by afternoon the river turned away completely from the forest and soon mostly tall grass surrounded them. Once in awhile bluffs of short, stunted leaf-trees would break up the landscape.

There were plenty of animals grazing in the grass-covered prairie. Herds of what looked like deer bolted away when the small caravan came too close.

The sun hung close to the horizon, when they came upon a tributary that flowed into the river they had been following. The road paralleled the new river for awhile until they came to a narrow, wooden bridge. They crossed it one wagon at a time. It didn't look too solid and Beringer gave a sigh of relief when everybody arrived safely on the other side.

Soon after that they came upon a fork in the road, one leg followed the old river; the one they chose veered sharply to the right, away from the river. It led toward a small forest.

"The Ballard-creek farm is just beyond that forest," Aran explained to Beringer. "We should be there before sunset."

The road they were on seemed wider, more frequently traveled.

Suddenly the wagon stopped, shouting came from the front of the wagon-train. Beringer guided his horse to the front. Esram climbed down from his wagon, carrying something that looked like a crossbow in his hand.

Beringer wondered briefly about such an antique weapon, but didn't have much time to dwell on it. The road had opened into a large glade, with a pond to the right. What he saw on the water's surface made even Beringer hold his breath.

In its center floated one of the Xandra-plants, a *water-lily*. At one time it had been a living plant. Now only a mass of chopped-up plant matter remained. All around it floated a number of giant pods, split open, filled with the bloody remains of what once had been human bodies.

Unborn Xandra-Humans.

"Raiders!" Esram said between clenched teeth. "I'm afraid of what we'll find at the farm."

"This looks fresh," said one of Esram's sons.

"Probably happened early this morning," another one said.

Beringer noticed that all the men were armed with long-barreled guns.

"They might still be around," warned Esram. He turned to one of his sons. "Orsam, you ride ahead, scout out the area. And be careful."

Orsam dug his heels into his horse's flanks and took off.

Esram looked at Beringer. "If you have a weapon, get it ready. There may be violence."

"He has a gun that throws bolts of lightning," Aran said. "That's how he killed the bounty-hunters."

"Bolts of lightning!" Esram stared with narrow eyes. "There are stories about such weapons, which our ancestors possessed, but only soldiers were allowed to carry them. All got lost over time. How would you come into possession of a weapon like that?"

"We never lost them," Beringer said. "It is my right to carry one. I am a soldier."

"There is much you have to tell me," Esram mused. "I think you are a man of many stories. I am very interested in the place where you come from."

Chapter Seventeen

They were still there, the raiders. Beringer counted eleven horses. He didn't see any guards. From inside the house came loud voices, shouts and laughter.

Beringer studied the house. It felt like stepping back in time. He had only seen houses like this on paintings hanging in museums back on Earth. The house looked quite large, two stories high, with rows of small windows on each floor. The walls were constructed from a combination of clay-bricks and wood.

Behind the house stood a couple of smaller buildings, most likely they held life-stock. Beringer heard the bleating of some kind of animal. In the dirt-trampled yard in front of the house he saw what he recognized as fowl.

He also saw two lifeless bodies not far from the house, one the body of a woman. She had been stripped of her clothing. From her belly strutted a wooden stake.

The other one that of a young boy, his twisted body lay in a bloody heap beside the woman.

Beringer gritted his teeth. A soldier is used to bloodshed, but it is easy to push a button and watch the explosion on a computer screen. Even when you know you just killed maybe a few dozen people, usually soldiers or mercenaries, it is not hard to detach yourself. They are faceless, nameless men you've never seen or met, just numbers, statistics.

This was different. These were real people.

A child and a woman.

Brutally murdered.

He looked at Esram, who squatted beside him. "You knew these people?"

The old man nodded. "My cousin," he said, his voice almost a whisper, but Beringer heard the agony, the anger.

Starmote appeared beside Beringer, she held a device in her hand, pointed it at the house. "There are sixteen life-forms inside," she said. Beringer glanced at the device, alien to him. "Any signs of life?" he asked.

"Two are dead, one unconscious, all three are males. Two females, alive, and eleven males, also alive." She spoke quietly, so only Beringer could hear.

"We could go in shooting," Esram said, "but if anyone is still alive they would surely be killed by the raiders."

"There is no need for bloodshed," Starmote said. "I could fire a gas-pellet through that open window. It would put everyone to sleep."

"Do it!" Beringer said without hesitation. He watched her pull a small tube out of one of her belt-pouches. She aimed it at the window she had indicated. He heard a barely audible whispering sound, and then he saw her put the tube back into her pouch. Not for the first time Beringer wondered what other weapons she carried.

"It is done," she said, looking at her device. "They are all unconscious."

The laughter and shouting had stopped. The sudden silence became almost unnerving.

Esram didn't quite trust Starmote's evaluation of the situation. "Maybe they know we are here," he said.

Starmote shook her head. "They won't be out for long, you better act now," she suggested.

Esram spoke to one of his sons. "You, Robar, go and investigate. Take one of the hounds. We'll cover you."

Robar nodded. Rifle gripped tightly in his hand, he made his way cautiously toward the house, taking cover behind every tree. The huge hound followed like a silent shadow close on his heels. Robar walked up the wooden stairs, crept along the wall toward the entrance. Listening for movement, he finally opened the door slowly, stepped inside the house. Moments later he came back, shouted, "It is safe. They're all unconscious."

The group rushed toward the house. Beringer and Starmote followed slowly. Before they even reached the stairs a couple of Esram's sons dragged the body of a man onto the veranda, then down the steps. Unceremoniously they dumped him onto the ground and went back to get another one.

Soon eleven unconscious men lay in the dirt. All of them wore leather breeches and short leather coats. Most of the men sprouted beards. Two of them had only a mustache. Both men looked fairly young.

Esram came walking down the stairs, stood wide-legged in front of the men on the ground. He cursed suddenly, spit, and kicked one of them in the ribs. The man lay naked from the waist down, blood gushing from his slit throat.

Looking up, Esram stared at Robar. "Let the hounds have them," he said, his voice sending a chill down Beringer's back.

When Starmote took a step forward, he held her back. "They have their own justice. We can't interfere."

Robar spoke to the hounds who had been watching with glittering eyes, saliva dripping from their jowls. With a roar the four huge animals began their grisly job, tearing out throats and ripping entrails from living bodies. Fountains of blood spurted everywhere. Soon the shaggy coats of the hounds were matted and red.

Beringer turned away. "It might have been more merciful had you killed them outright. Come, let's go into the house," he said to Starmote.

They stepped through the doorway into a large room, clearly a kitchen and dining area. Food covered one of the two large tables in the dining area. The other table caught Beringer's attention.

A naked woman lay on top of the table, her legs still spread apart. She was either unconscious or dead.

Esram saw Beringer look. "My cousin," he said. "One of those Xandra-cursed animals lay still on top of her when we came in. Too bad he wasn't conscious so he could feel my knife when I slit his throat." He walked to the table, gently closed the woman's thighs.

One of Esram's sons came down the stairs which led to the upper floor. He carried a young woman in his arms. He laid her gently on a mat on the floor, took off his shirt and covered her naked body. "Helgie is alive, but not unharmed," he said, his face grim and his young eyes hard. "We should have let them wake up first before we set the hounds to work."

Aran came out of one of the rooms on the main floor. "Brakko and Nelto are dead. Brico is alive, but hurt. He needs medical attention."

"I'll see what I can do," Starmote offered her help and followed Aran back into the room.

"Robar, Stark, and Elia, go get the wagons and the women. We'll spend the night here, as planned," Esram ordered three of his sons. They nodded and left.

The woman on the table began to stir, opened her eyes and started screaming. When her eyes focused on Esram, who stood bent over her, she stopped screaming, sat up and flung her arms around his neck. He padded her back, held her for a moment, while she clung to him, sobbing loudly. He removed her arms gently. "It's alright, Quirma." He spoke soothingly. "You are safe now."

With wild eyes she looked around the room, spotted the girl on the floor. "Oh, Helgie," she cried out, "what have they done to you?"

Esram held her arm. "She is alive, Quirma."

"Thank the Xandra. What about the others? I know Brakko is dead, they shot him. Where is Nelto, where is Brico?"

"Brico is alive, wounded, but alive. Nelto--I'm afraid he is also dead."

"Oh no, not Nelto, he was my favorite little brother. And Keltie and little Corba? You said nothing about them."

"Dead." Esram said.

Before he could say more the door flew open and Myra, his wife, rushed in. When she saw Quirma she began to sob, ran to the table and took the other woman into her arms. "I saw Corba outside, and Keltie. How could they do such an awful thing?"

Starmote came out of the room she had been in, she looked at Beringer. "I treated his wounds as best as I could," she said. "He got shot with some kind of projectile weapon, once in the leg and once in his shoulder. He should consider himself lucky; his ribs deflected one of the shots."

"I guess there is nothing else we can do in here," Beringer said. "I'd like to go and talk to Lt. Wang. I suggest we leave these people alone for awhile."

Starmote nodded, followed him out of the door. A horrible scene greeted them outside. The hounds had literally torn the bodies of the raiders apart. Body parts were scattered everywhere across the blood-soaked ground.

Beringer shook his head. He didn't care about the raiders being killed, they deserved it, but he would have preferred a less messy method.

The rest of their party arrived in the slowly gathering darkness. Someone lit some torches and in their flickering light Beringer saw Vic and Torka, the two Xandra-born men, helping Lt. Wang with the horses. He also noticed that most of the girls were busy rubbing down their animals. He walked over to his lieutenant, while Starmote went to check on Mirna and her baby son.

Wang looked up from his task when he heard Beringer approaching. "Commander," he said, acknowledging his presence.

Beringer tipped his cap in a sloppy salute. "Everything under control?" he asked.

Wang smiled faintly. "I see I missed all the action," he said, "these people play rough."

"It's a brutal place." Beringer watched Wang rub down his horse with some kind of brush. "You seem to have a knack for this, Lieutenant," he commented, smiled and added, "I want to have a closer look at the coats those raiders wore. Or what's left of them. Care to join me?"

Both men walked over to the spot where the carnage had taken place. Wang didn't say anything, but Beringer could see the disapproval in the young man's face. "Don't you find it peculiar that all these men wore the same type of coat?"

Wang picked up a shredded piece of leather, held the bloodstained material into the light, studying the faded outline of the crude drawing of a rifle and a sword crossing each other inside a circle.

Beringer picked up another piece, it held the same drawing. "Looks like some kind of emblem," he said.

Wang found a coat miraculously almost intact, except for the ripped-off sleeve. When he gave the coat a shake the emblem could clearly be seen on its back. He threw Beringer a thoughtful look. "I don't think these were ordinary raiders. They belonged to some kind of organization. Military, perhaps?"

"I am thinking along the same lines. I saw their rifles inside the house. Primitive projectile weapons, but they had military written all over them," Beringer said. "We may have stumbled into a war," Wang said quietly. "Which side are we on?"

Beringer lifted his eyes toward the sky. The silver disks of the two satellites rose above the tree tops, illuminating the farm house and yard. In their harsh light the bloody chunks of meat that had once been breathing human beings looked unreal, like pieces of statues, scattered by a mad artist. "Someone should clean this up," Beringer said, more to himself than to his lieutenant.

"The night-scavengers will take care of it," said a fierce female voice behind them.

Beringer turned to see Mirna standing there. In her arms she held a small child, her baby-boy. When he saw Beringer looking at him, he gurgled happily, gave him a big smile and waved a pudgy little hand in the air. *The ignorance of a child*, Beringer thought. *It is so precious. Some day you'll be holding a weapon in your hands, taking another's life.* He reached out and touched the boy gently on the nose. "He's beautiful. I love those big brown eyes," he said to Mirna.

The girl, Beringer could think of her only in those terms, because of her young age, smiled. "His name is Dorn. He takes after his father. Rolard is a gentle man. He hates all violence. I hope Dorn grows up like him." She sighed. "Unfortunately, violence is part of our world, and it is hard to survive if you are soft." She looked at the house. "My brothers told me what happened in there. I better go in and talk to Helgie. She is not much older than I am. Now she'll have to carry the bastard-child of a raider. This is so awful." She gathered her son closer to her breast and hurried toward the house.

"She can't be any more than sixteen *Norm-Years,"* Lt. Wang said beside Beringer, "and a mother already."

"She'll probably have four kids before she's twenty," Beringer commented, remembering the way she had pulled up her dress when she'd seen him looking at her at breakfast.

A couple of the men came out of the house. They walked over to an outbuilding and pushed out a small wagon. One of them got one of the horses and hitched it in front of the wagon. He pulled up beside Beringer and Wang, who had been watching. "Can you give us a hand loading up these bodies?" he asked Beringer.

They threw the body parts onto the wagon. Beringer and Wang put their nose-filters in place because of the nauseating stench. When they were finished, the two brothers took the wagon with its grisly load into the fields, away from the house. Beringer, who had found a pump beside the house, was just washing his hands and face when they came back. Only the horse came back with them, they had left the wagon in the field.

Mirna stuck her head out of the door. "Supper will be ready in awhile. Would you come in, please."

Beringer didn't really feel hungry, but decided to go in anyway. He wanted to talk to Esram. But before he went inside, he needed to do something else. "Go ahead," he told Wang, "I just want to check in with Lambert."

When he spoke the coded numbers that would trigger the connection to the shuttle nothing happened.

There was no response.

Chapter Eighteen

Lambert watched Commander Beringer and his small team on the screen. They disappeared from view as they entered a path leading into the forest. He sighed and got up from his seat. He secured the door. Then stretched out on one of the cots in the sleeping quarters. He didn't worry, if anything should approach the shuttle, the computer would trigger an alarm.

Strange to see trees and vegetation in their natural environment. Just knowing that the shuttle sat in the middle of a jungle on an alien planet sent small shivers up his spine.

He had never been on the surface of a planet, never breathed real air. Born and growing up on Ganymede, one of Jupiter's moons, he knew only artificial air, artificially grown food and vegetation.

After joining the space navy he spent his adult life on various ships and space-stations.

He had to admit to himself, he felt a little afraid of opening the door and stepping outside. Sighing again, he relaxed. He saw no reason to even waste time thinking about that possibility. He needed to stay put and wait for the Commander's orders, should he require assistance.

In the morning, he sat dutifully in front of the screen, watching the surrounding area. The day went by without anything significant happening, except for the group of small, kangaroo-like animals that hopped into the clearing to graze for awhile. When night fell, he lay down again on his cot, began to daydream.

Not being aware of falling asleep, the screaming alarm jolted him awake, leaving him momentarily disoriented. Jumping up, he rushed into the control room. The shuttle's sensors displayed the outside world on the large screen as a three-dimensional image, creating the illusion of being outside. Whatever approached the shuttle triggered the floodlights. Lambert stared disbelieving at the screen.

Two girls stood beside the pond, facing the shuttle and waving. Both girls were naked, both were beautiful.

He noticed their high, full breasts, their long black hair, but he also noticed the large alien eyes.

"Alarm off," he told the computer and ordered, "Outside audio."

Only one of the girls talked. He didn't know what language she spoke, but it didn't matter, because the device behind his ear translated it automatically.

"Traveler from another world," came the clear voice, "come out of your vessel and join us. My sister and I are eager to welcome you to our world."

Lambert studied the screen. The pond behind them seemed quiet, only one large plant floated in its center. Looking at the small screen, which displayed a panorama of the outside, he saw nothing threatening. He knew his orders were not leave the shuttle, but what harm would it do to go and talk to those girls?

They came closer. Both of them smiled and ran their hands down their bodies. They looked so exquisite and inviting.

"Come," one of them said, "we are waiting." Their beautiful bodies swayed as they came closer.

Without thought he gave the door the command to open. Cool, humid air entered the shuttle. He inhaled deeply, filled his lungs with air not artificially produced. He detected a strange, exotic fragrance, became slightly heady as the pheromones invaded his body.

He stepped onto the mat of green grass. Looking into the night sky, without the aid of artificial instrument, he saw the two bright disks of the planet's satellites. They looked strange and beautiful.

A soft hand touched his. He stared into a pair of large purple eyes.

"I am Virni," the alien girl said.

"And I am Sirsi," said the second one and took his other hand.

"Come," Virni said and smiled up at him. "Sirsi and I will collect your seed for the Mother."

They pulled him gently toward the pond. Virni lay down in the grass under one of the tall trees, her legs apart. Sirsi began tugging on his shirt. He opened his belt with flying fingers and let Sirsi pull down his trousers. His penis already painfully stiff, he dropped to his knees, and with a muffled cry he moved between Virni's widespread thighs.

He could see her pink slit clearly between her puffed hairless lips, and without preliminaries he pushed his pole into her. The moment he entered her soft, tight sex-canal waves of pure pleasure washed through his body.

He moved like a berserker between the alien girl's clutching thighs. His need had been so great that he erupted in a very short time. Roaring, he emptied himself into the warm vessel and collapsed on top of the girl. Virni stroked his head. He looked into her purple eyes. She smiled and then she kissed him. He felt her tongue enter his open mouth and began to suck on it.

Warm liquid filled his mouth, he swallowed. It tasted like warm honey. He became aware of her softly pulsing sheath and felt his penis harden. Virni broke the kiss, offered him her breast. Like a starving infant he sucked the long thick nipple into his mouth and drank from the sweet nectar that flowed from it.

Feeling strong and virile, like he had never felt before, he began to move with a steady rhythm. The alien vagina caressed his swollen member, sending waves and waves of unbelievable pleasure into his brain.

Soft, strong hands tugged on his hips. He let himself be pulled up, momentarily disappointed when his stiff penis slipped out of Virnis's clutching organ. Sirsi, the other girl, pushed him onto his back and straddled him. He watched with anticipation as another hot vessel swallowed up his pole, fascinated by the way the puffed lips molded themselves around his shaft. He moaned loudly when the pleasure began.

His eyes were glued to Sirsi's large, full breasts. They barely moved as she bounced and gyrated above him. She made him come inside her, sucked up his sperm. Then she lifted up, but before he could complain, Virni lowered herself onto his strutting member. Her large purple eyes locked with his. Her laughter sounded high and child-like when he erupted again inside her.

Virni and Sirsi changed places above him many times; after awhile he couldn't tell them apart anymore. It didn't matter. Both of them gave him pleasures beyond anything he had ever experienced. Both fed him their honey-nectar that lent him strength and endurance.

When they were finished with him, he lay on his belly, watching them peel something shiny from between their legs and put it into the water.

His mind began to clear and he noticed for the first time how much these two girls resembled the Genaar-females.

He watched them swimming in the water, listened to their silvery laughter and admired their slim, well formed bodies. Then he turned onto his back and stared into the sky. The two moons had drifted apart, a third one had joined them in the night-sky. It bathed the pond with reddish light. He became suddenly aware that the flood lights from the shuttle had turned themselves off.

He felt strange, knowing that no artificial shield existed between him and space. The sky seemed to go on forever and the satellites looked different seen through a layer of air.

Ganymede didn't have its own air, and the artificially produced stuff inside the domes had never smelled like this. He closed his eyes, inhaled deeply, letting the humid air trickle through his nose and into his lungs.

When a soft hand touched his shoulder, he opened his eyes lazily and looked into a pair of purple eyes. "Virni?" he asked.

The girl shook her head, straddled him. Looking at her swollen hairless mons, he reacted immediately. Her hand grabbed his stiff mast, guided in toward her puffy lips. Then she sank down and took him deep inside her.

The pleasure raced through his body, but somehow his mind seemed much clearer now. She smiled, then laughed throatily, not childlike as before.

"You have not been with a woman for a long time," she said, making it a statement, not a question.

He nodded. "No," he breathed, "and never with one like you."

"I know," she said and began to pump her hips back and forth.

As he approached his orgasm he became aware that the girl above him had changed. Her hair had become long and flowing and the color of dark blood. And her eyes, they were different, too, no longer alien. Still purple, but human looking.

When he erupted inside her, she stretched out on top of him. Her large breasts lay soft against his heaving chest. Her red lips clamped over his, from her open mouth flowed sweet, thick nectar. It ran down his throat, like hot fire.

"I am *The Xandra*," she said inside his head. "Your mind is open to me. I know what you know."

His climax seemed to go on forever.

When he regained his senses, he found himself alone. Sitting up, he lifted his face toward the bright sky. The alien sun, already halfway to its zenith, warmed his naked skin. Looking around he discovered his clothing in a rumpled heap not far away.

Not a ripple disturbed the still water of the pond. In its center the large floating plant looked like a huge, beautiful purple rose.

Fragments of ghostly memories popped into his mind. He saw the face of a beautiful woman with long red hair, saw her undulating white body, heard the whisper of her voice.

He rubbed his eyes. Had he been hallucinating?

He got up, dressed. Then he noticed that the door to the shuttle was open.

Damn it! He had to be more careful. The Commander must not hear about this.

He didn't put on his boots. He carried them in his hands and slowly walked back to the shuttle, enjoying the feel of the soft grass underneath his naked feed. Taking a deep breath, he relished the smell of the fresh air. Back in the shuttle, he closed the door with reluctance. The air inside the shuttle seemed suddenly stale and sterile. He envied Beringer and the others. How excited they must be walking across a strange and alien landscape.

He broke open some rations, ate with little enthusiasm. Outside, he had seen some bright red fruit hanging from the trees. It would have been a treat to eat some of those. But, of course, he could not take a chance, without having them tested first. The most beautiful things can also be the most deadly.

He saw those small kangaroo-like animals again, watched them jump around with fascination. Wild animals in their natural habitat! He had never seen anything like it.

He witnessed one shocking incident, and it left him shaken up.

One of the small creatures entered the water, swam toward the floating plant. Somehow it managed to pull itself up onto the plant. It hopped into the plant's center and began to sniff at something.

Then it happened!

A mass of long, thick tendrils shot out of the plant. They wrapped themselves around the little animal and disappeared back into the plant, taking their victim with them.

Lucky I didn't want to go for a swim, Lambert thought, *that could have been me.*

In the evening, he sat in front of the screen, watching the clearing and the pond with anticipation. The flood lights illuminated everything quite clearly. Nothing could come and go undetected.

He must have dozed off. Suddenly they were there.

Two naked girls. Seeing them triggered the memory of the previous night.

Only one of them came closer. Over his speakers he heard her calling. "Come out, John Lambert, the Mother needs you." She waved and raised her voice. "John Lambert, come out."

How did she know his name? Reluctantly, he decided to take another chance. The memory of the small *kangaroo* made him wonder if he might be the plant's next meal. Outside, he again detected the heady fragrance in the air. Looking at the nude slim body of the girl, a longing desire to take her into his arms suddenly gripped him.

She smiled, stepped closer. When he tried to put his arms around her, she put her small hands against his chest. "No seed-collecting tonight," she said, quite firmly, but added with a little smile, "Maybe later."

"But I need you," he stammered hoarsely.

"I have a message from the Mother: John Lambert, take your shuttle and fly it to a place that is known to Virni, she will be your guide." She looked at Lambert. "That is the message. I will come with you."

"Hold it!" Lambert protested. "I have my orders. I can't just leave here."

"You must," the girl said urgently. "It is important." She lifted up, kissed him gently on the lips. "You will be in no danger. You are in the protection of the Mother."

"You keep mentioning the Mother. Who is she?"

The girl shrugged. "She is the Mother. She knows everything. She is everywhere. I am her daughter." She laughed in her childish way. "But I don't know much. Only when *She* touches me, then I know things."

Lambert shook his head. "I have absolutely no idea what you are talking about." He touched the girl's breast. Then he put his arm around her shoulder. He could feel his penis rising inside his pants.

"No seed-collecting," Virni said solemnly. "No time. Do it later." She pushed against him. "We must go now. There is very little time."

Reluctantly, he let her push him toward the shuttle. She hesitated a little before she stepped inside. Her large eyes seemed even larger when she looked around. She clasped her hands when she saw the big screen and laughed. "The Mother told me about the window inside your flying egg. There I will find the place we have to go to."

"I wondered about that." Lambert said and slid into the pilot's seat. "Come," he said to Virni. "Sit next to me."

Gingerly, the girl sat down.

"Well?" Lambert looked at Virni.

"I know that you have a map of the continents in your databanks," the girl said. "Bring it up on the screen."

Lambert gave her a sharp look. Her voice sounded different, not timid and childlike, but full and throaty.

She laughed when she saw his look.

122

"You're not Virni," he said.

"I am *The Xandra*. I am using Virni's body as a vessel to communicate with you." She smiled. "You remember me."

When she touched his mind he almost cried out. He remembered. He saw long red hair swirling around a voluptuous undulating body. He felt the fire racing through his system. Then the vision disappeared. He stared at the young girl in the seat next to him. "It was no dream, then," he breathed.

"No dream." She nodded. "You see, I could force you to do my bidding, but I choose not to. Now, display part of the northern continent."

Lambert attached the *command-interface* discs to his temples. The picture changed. The girl studied the map for a moment. Then she pointed to a spot. "There," she said. "I want you to go there."

"That's about five hundred kilometers from here," Lambert said.

"Five hundred and seventeen, to be exact. You should be there within thirty minutes. You'll know what to do when you get there. Then come back to this location." She pointed to another spot.

"Looks close by."

"It is. I'll be waiting there for you. Go now." She looked into his eyes. "I am counting on you, John Lambert."

Lambert stared at the screen. Red dots appeared on the indicated spots, and then the map was gone. In its place the pond and the clearing appeared on the screen. Sirsi still stood beside the pond.

"What about her. Should she come, too?" Lambert asked.

"Only I am needed." Virni said in her old voice. She settled into the seat. "We must hurry now."

Lambert didn't comment and concentrated on the computer. The shuttle lifted silently, the pond on the screen became small, and then the screen displayed only a mass of tree-tops that moved with ever increasing speed. Sometimes the trees thinned out and they flew over grass-covered prairie. Once they crossed a wide river. Even though it was dark outside, the picture on the computer screen stayed bright and clear.

Beside Lambert the girl sat quiet, her large purple eyes glued to the moving landscape on the screen.

Lambert watched her somewhat bemused. Obviously, she had never flown before, but she didn't seem scared. Then again, except for the changing display on the screen, nothing indicated that the shuttle actually moved.

"Are you a Genaar?" Lambert asked the girl.

She looked at him. "I don't understand," she said.

"Where do you come from? Are there many like you? What do you call yourself?"

"I am Virni."

"I know, but what are your people called?"

She shook her head, not comprehending the question.

"Where do you live?" Lambert asked.

"In the forest, with my sisters."

"Do you live in a city, in a house, maybe?"

"I know about the City, but I don't live there. My house is small. It is built from the branches of a tree." She touched the armrest of the chair she sat in and ran her fingers across the leather-like covering. "You have wondrous things in your house."

"This is not a house. It is a machine that flies high above the ground, very high. If I wanted to I could take you with me far away from here, right to the stars."

Virni laughed delightedly and clapped her hands together. "You are a *Star-child*. Did the *Star-gods* send you?" She reached out and touched his clothing. "You cover your body, why?"

Lambert shrugged. "Many reasons. Protection for one thing, modesty is another."

"I never wear clothing." Virni said and stroked her breasts.

"That's a beautiful necklace you are wearing," Lambert commented, staring at the pendant between her full breasts.

"Do you like it? I made it myself from stones, which I found while diving in the pond." She slipped it over her head and held it out toward Lambert. "Here," she said, "it is my gift to you."

Lambert took it, studied it. "These are precious stones," he said. "This could be worth a fortune." He looked at Virni. "Are you sure?" he asked.

She laughed. "I can make another. It means nothing to me."

Chapter Nineteen

Lambert looked at the displayed picture on the descending shuttle's screen and cursed loudly.

There on the ground lay a half-naked man. Blood covered his chest and the crushed half of his face. "His name is Viran," Virni said beside him. "The Mother wants you to bring him to the Sacred Valley."

Lambert scanned the surrounding area. The computer detected animals and people nearby. Magnifying the image, Lambert saw a few tents and covered wagons. Everything seemed quiet. Surprised, he realized that the animals were horses. He had never seen horses before, except in holograms.

Strapping his belt with the laser around his waist, he gave the command to open the entrance door and stepped outside. He didn't need to turn on the floodlights, because the two moons above were bright enough to show him what he needed to see.

The man, Virni had called him *Viran*, lay at the edge of a lake. Even though Lambert approached him cautiously and slowly, his boots seemed dreadfully loud in the silence of the night. Only once he heard the roar of a distant night-hunter, near enough to make his adrenalin flow. Beside him, Virni walked on silent bare feet.

After reaching the motionless figure in the tall grass, Lambert crouched down to check for life-signs. The man seemed young, his large frame covered with corded muscles. His deep chest looked dark with crusted blood, concealing, Lambert suspected, a large wound. He needed to apply a bandage to keep the wound from opening when he moved the man.

Lambert winced when he looked at the man's face. At one time it had been handsome, now nothing more than a contorted mask remained, half of it a bloody mess of ripped flesh and splintered bone. The grass around him stained red with blood.

Incredibly, the man was still alive, but only barely. Judging by the injuries, Lambert didn't think he would live much longer.

"I have to go back to the shuttle," he told Virni, "his wound needs to be treated, or he'll die when we touch him."

Virni nodded, knelt beside Viran.

It didn't take long for Lambert to find the med-kit. He chose a gel-pouch, hoping that it still worked. After all, it had lain in the cold vacuum of space for a thousand years.

Taking a floater, he hurried back to the injured man, broke open the pouch and sprayed his chest with a fine mist. When it touched the skin it solidified and formed a thin layer of artificial skin, only a temporary treatment, but it would be sufficient.

He separated the floater tubes. With the portable stretcher expanded and fully inflated, he attached the tubes to the sides of the platform. "We have to roll him onto the stretcher," he told the girl.

"He is big," Virni said. "I am not very strong."

A loud flapping sound made Lambert look around. He jumped to his feet when he saw a large shadow, like a giant bird, outlined against the sky. Cursing, he reached for his laser.

As if sensing what he was about to do, Virni's fingers curled around his arm. "There is no danger," she said with a hurried voice. "It is only an *Angel*."

As the winged creature came closer, he saw that is was not a bird, but a human girl with wings. She landed in front of them, folded her wings and held up a hand. "I am Angela," she said.

Lambert stared at her fragile form, immediately smitten by her beautiful face.

The winged girl rushed to Viran's side, bent to touch him. She looked up at Lambert. The moonlight fell onto her face. He could see the tears in her large blue eyes. "I found him like this," she said. "But I could not help him. Can you help him?"

"The Mother can," Virni said beside Lambert. "We will take him to her."

"Help us get him onto the stretcher," Lambert said to the winged girl. He accepted her presence, nothing surprised him anymore. With Virni's and Angela's help Lambert managed to move the injured man onto the portable stretcher. He then activated the power unit. It lifted the floater with its heavy load slowly into the air. The girls helped him push the stretcher toward the shuttle.

They almost made it, when Lambert heard a sound, like someone sneezing. It came from the direction of the tents, except it seemed much closer. When he stared into the semi-darkness, he saw movement in the tall grass. "There is someone watching us," he said in a low voice to the girls.

Angela, who, obviously, had better eyes than Lambert, pointed with her finger. "Over there," she said, "a Human, in the grass."

The watcher jumped up when he saw Angela pointing at him and began running back toward the camp, shouting.

Men emerged from the tents, men carrying rifles. The rifles didn't look like anything Lambert had ever seen, but he didn't think that they were just sticks.

One of the men lifted his rifle to his cheek. The sharp crack of an explosion split the air. Beside Lambert the winged girl cried out, stumbled and fell to the ground. She lay on her belly. A dark stain appeared between her white wings.

Lambert cursed, whipped out his laser and aimed it at the big man who fired the shot, only a short distance away now and coming closer. Gritting his teeth, Lambert fired into the man's head and watched him collapse into the grass. He felt no remorse. They had been attacked, and by the looks of it the man killed the winged girl.

Another one of the men lifted his weapon. Lambert shot him in the chest. The other men stopped running and stood glaring at Lambert. None of them made any threatening moves.

"Why did you attack us?" Lambert shouted.

"It was Oron who attacked, not us," said one of them.

"Why did he?"

The man, who had spoken, shrugged. "He doesn't like anyone interfere with his property."

Lambert looked grimly at the lifeless heap in the tall grass. "He won't have to worry about that anymore. He's dead."

"It would have happened sooner or later," the man said. "He won't be mourned."

Lambert studied the men who confronted him. They were a wild, menacing looking group, sprouting beards and wearing brown, loose robes, which had seen better days.

"That is a strange weapon you have there," the man said. "I've never seen a weapon like that. Who are you?"

"I am John Lambert. I am a marine with the *Terran Space Navy*. And who are you?"

"My name is Wiams and I am just a simple trader. We all are." He smiled and made a sweeping gesture toward his companions, who seemed to watch Lambert like vultures watching a dying victim.

Lambert kept his weapon in his hand. "I will take my friends into the shuttle," he said. "I hope I will be able do so unmolested."

"You have strange friends." The man had come a little closer. "An *Angel* and a *Water-Nymph*. Are you *Xandra-born*?" he asked.

"I don't know what you mean. I am a stranger and I am just helping someone who needed help." Lambert waved his laser. "Don't come any closer," he warned the man. "I will not hesitate to use this again!"

He looked past the watching men when he heard some yelling coming from the wagons. Then he saw two figures running away from the wagons, toward him.

Two women. Two naked women.

One dark-haired, the other blond, almost white. When they came closer, he noticed that both women wore their hair close-cropped to the skull, military style.

"Take us with you," the older one pleaded. "We are prisoners."

"Prisoners?" Lambert eyed her with suspicion. "Is this some kind of trick to get onto my shuttle?"

"No trick," said the blonde one. "Whoever you are, please, take us away from this stinking hell hole." She looked at Viran on the stretcher. "He is our friend," she said with a low voice. "We would appreciate it if you would let us accompany him." Then she looked at the prone figure of the winged girl, seeing her for the first time. Gasping, she said, "That is Angela. Is she dead?"

"I don't know. Why don't you check her?"

The blond girl crouched down beside Angela. "She is alive," she announced, "but unconscious. And she is bleeding. She needs medical attention, fast."

"Can you and your friend carry her into the shuttle?"

The girl nodded. The dark-haired one also knelt beside Angela now and very carefully she lifted one of the wings. "These antique weapons can do a lot of damage," she said to the blond girl, her gray eyes grave. With a low voice she added, "I don't think she's going to make it."

"Are you a doctor?" Lambert asked her.

"I could be one if I had the right instruments," the woman answered. She looked at her companion. "Come, let's put her inside." Together they carried Angela into the shuttle. Virni helped Lambert to push the stretcher through the entrance. Once inside Lambert gave the order to seal the door.

"Lift off," he told the computer. "Destination *Beta.*"

Once in the air, he pushed the stretcher into the sleeping quarters. The two women had already put the winged girl onto one of the bunk-beds.

"Do you have any medical supplies?" the dark-haired woman asked.

"I'll get you the med-kit," Lambert said.

Virni sat in the co-pilot's seat, watching the screen. She smiled at Lambert when he walked in. "The Mother will be pleased with you. Everything is alright now."

"I hope so." Lambert took the small med-kit from its storage compartment, went back into the other room.

The older woman looked at the contents and shook her head. "Where are your scanners? Don't you have any wavers or micro-beamers? They are basic components of every med-doc."

"I don't even know what those things are" Lambert shrugged. "They didn't equip these shuttles with the latest in medical discoveries. Only exploration vehicles carry a full med-doc."

"I'll say. There is nothing in here that I even recognize. What are all these jelly-filled pouches?"

"That's artificial skin. You break them open and the stuff comes out in a fine mist. I guess they don't have that where you come from?"

The woman snorted. "It's primitive." She sighed and looked at the blond girl. "We should have gone back and taken our clothes and our equipment." She brushed her hand over her short, black hair, wrinkled her nose. "I must look awful," she said, suddenly conscious of her nudity. "My name is Mirtin, and *Blue-Eyes* here calls herself Vienne."

Lambert gave them a curt nod. "I am John Lambert. By the way, I never did get where you ladies hail from."

"We never said." Mirtin smiled. "Let me ask you a question. Are you native to this… this world?"

"Isn't it obvious?" Lambert didn't give her a direct answer. "How about you?"

"You might say we are explorers." Mirtin said with a calculating look in her eyes. "What exactly are you doing here?"

"I guess I am an explorer as well," Lambert answered. "Look, I am a little uncomfortable surrounded by all you naked females. I think you'll find some outfits in those lockers. They may not be an exact fit." He shrugged. "Unless you are used to running around in the nude."

"A bath would be nice," Vienne said.

"Sorry, can't oblige you there." Lambert looked at Viran on the stretcher. "Poor bastard. You said he is your friend. What happened?"

"He got himself shot by the man you killed," Mirtin told him. "We didn't see it happen, but we heard the shot. There was nothing we could have done."

"What is he to you?" Lambert asked.

"Nothing, really. He was our guide," Mirtin admitted. "But we owe him, he saved our lives."

While the two women rummaged through the lockers for something to wear, Lambert went back into the control-cabin and sank into the pilot's seat. He could really do nothing. The computer controlled the flight of the shuttle. "How long until we land?" he asked the computer.

"The shuttle will land in five minutes and twenty five seconds." The computer spoke with a pleasant female voice.

"Where is your companion?" Virni, who had been watching, asked beside him.

"Who?"

"The one who speaks to you."

"Oh." Lambert chuckled. "That is not a person. It's a machine."

"What is a *machine*?"

"A machine is something that we build. It does things, like...moving stuff, or...lets see...this shuttle we are in is a machine. I can't really explain it in easy terms. I never thought about it. Machines are just... machines."

"If machines can talk like people, can they look like people?"

Lambert gave Virni a thoughtful look. This girl seemed to be more complicated and intelligent than she appeared to be.

"We've built machines that looked like people and acted like people, but not anymore. They used to call them robots, androids, artificials, and a host of other names. Until somebody decided it was not right. Why create artificial people when it is so easy to produce them naturally." He grinned. "And more fun."

Virni laughed. Obviously, she hadn't understood a word. She was an alien. He knew nothing about her and this planet. Commander Beringer had not briefed him.

He spent a thousand years in cryogenic suspension. In a way it didn't seem real, for him it had only been a few weeks since Beringer gave the command to abandon the tower and join the alien Genaar in the bowels of the space station. None of the men were given a reason. There were plenty of rumors. He knew that the planet Nu-Eden had been put under quarantine. Now here he was, a thousand years later, on the surface of the same planet, involved in something he had no control over.

The computer's voice interrupted his thoughts. "The shuttle has touched down."

He looked at the screen. He saw buildings outside. They looked old and weathered, but without a doubt, built by Humans.

He also saw people.

When he opened the door, he noticed that it was still night outside. A third moon rose above the cliffs that surrounded a large valley. He saw the reflection in the dark water of a lake. The buildings he had seen on the screen lay in darkness, in the shadow of tall trees.

"Welcome to my sanctuary, John Lambert," said a soft, familiar voice. When he looked he saw a tall woman with long, flaming red hair and deep green eyes, dressed in a loose, white, flowing robe.

"It is you," he said hoarsely. "You are real."

She laughed throatily. "You remember me."

"Who are you?" Lambert asked, as images of her naked body gyrating above him, and ghostly memories of pleasures beyond belief, flashed through his mind.

"I am *The Xandra*," she said. "But time for questions later, there are more important matters to attend to now."

A couple of large, muscular men stepped out of the shadows, climbed up the stairs into the shuttle. Lambert moved aside to let them pass. "In there," he said. They didn't speak, just walked into the other room. When they came back out, one carried Viran, as if he were a child; the other one brought the winged girl.

Lambert watched them carry their burdens away toward a grove of trees. "What will happen to them?" he asked the woman.

"I will restore them," the Xandra answered, "but, now, come and let me show you the Sacred Valley. Your friends are welcome to join us." She turned to Virni, who stood looking forlorn beside Lambert. "You have done well, my daughter. I will have one of my guards take you back to your own nest."

Virni took the Xandra's hand and kissed it. "Thank you, Great Mother," she said.

The Xandra looked into the sky. The two silvery moons were dipping toward the horizon, the third one burned like a red eye on a speckled black canvas. "Not much time left until dawn," she said. "But enough time to show you around."

Even though everything Lambert saw showed great age, he saw no debris lying around. The tiled terrace they walked on had been swept clean of fallen leaves and dirt. The Xandra led Lambert toward a tall stone statue.

Lambert looked at the statue of a handsome, fairly muscular man of undetermined age. He stood with his arms folded in front of his chest, his gaze toward the heavens. Lambert bent closer to read the inscription on the weathered plaque at the base of the statue.

THOMAS PATRICK McCLARY. HUMAN.

The Xandra smiled. "If I ever truly loved a man, it was Tom McClary. He was the first human whose mind and body joined with mine. For a little while I made him a god." She looked suddenly sad. "I had a dream, but things went wrong. You Humans call my world Nu-Eden, Paradise. It could have been, but I misjudged the human animal. Humans are more complex than I had realized. More cunning, more evil. Tom McClary had a good, honest mind, but not all Humans are like him." She laughed suddenly, hooked her arm into Lambert's. "I have looked into your mind, John Lambert. You are much like Tom."

As Lambert walked beside her a sudden thought struck him. "You look different," he said. "I remember your deep purple eyes, now they are green."

Her laughter sounded soft, deep throated. "The woman you remember was another manifestation of mine. I am The Xandra. I can be in many places at the same time. You know nothing about me, don't you, John Lambert?"

He shook his head. "Obviously not as much as you know about me."

She stopped and looked into his eyes. Her eyes were large, and in the light of the red moon they glowed with a deep green fire. "I know everything about you, John. I also know about Commander Beringer and the others who are trying to gather information about me and my world. I know that you spent a thousand of your years frozen in the space-station of the Genaar. Yes, I know about them, too. More than you think. You want to know who and what I am? I am The Xandra, the Mother of Light. I am the ruler of this world. I am a goddess." Her eyes and voice softened when she said, "I am not evil. The evil came to my world." She pulled on his arm. "Come, let's go inside."

Lambert had completely forgotten about the two women he had rescued. He turned to look for them. Both of them were still standing beside the statue of Thomas McClary, studying and discussing it, or so it seemed to Lambert. He couldn't hear what they were saying. They were talking in hushed voices.

The Xandra saw him looking. "They are strangers to my world, just like you, John Lambert. They represent an unknown factor. I know very little about them."

"They look harmless enough," Lambert said.

The woman smiled. "Never underestimate your fellow players, John. These two may seem harmless, but what about the force they might represent? Who are they? Where do they come from?"

Lambert shrugged. "I didn't have much time to think about them. They told me they were the injured man's friends."

"Viran rescued them from certain death, but they never were his friends, least of them Vienne, the blond one." The Xandra laughed. "She didn't like men, until she met Viran. Now she is confused. Let them be, I want to show you something."

The house they entered had stone walls, weathered and overgrown with climbing vines. It had no door, just a large, oval opening. At one time it might have had a curtain to keep out drafts, but now it stood open to the elements. The same proved true for the windows, no glass, only round open holes. The floors inside were covered with flat stones, laid neatly into the ground.

Every room looked clean, but void of any furnishings, except for the faded murals on the walls.

"Nobody lives here," Lambert stated.

"Not anymore, not for a long time, but I keep it preserved. This used to be the home of Thomas McClary, his wife Anina and his companions Mabel and Sister Angela. They lived here for almost a hundred of your years. Tom had children with all three women, twenty three sons and nineteen daughters."

"A busy man," Lambert commented dryly.

"He loved all three of them. When I brought them here I took away much of their memories. I thought it best. Later I realized that without their memories they were not whole, but shallow, like my creations. I gave them back what I had taken from them, or most of it. At first they were distraught, unhappy, and angry. I couldn't send them back to their own people. The ones they knew were not the same, I changed them. And the other colonists, the ones I let live their normal lives, they were strangers."

Lambert didn't really listen to her. The murals on the walls captured his attention. Most of them were of a religious nature, of angels and demons, gods and goddesses. Some depicted were-wolves, unicorns, dragons and creatures Lambert had never heard of.

"Who was the artist?" he asked.

"Sister Angela. She was a very talented human being." The Xandra smiled. "Many of my creations were born in her mind."

"I would like to look at these during daylight," Lambert said and chuckled. "I don't see too well in the dark."

"You Humans, you have so many handicaps. It is hard to comprehend how a race like yours achieved the things you have. By the way, I could change your eyes."

Lambert lifted a hand in a defensive gesture. "No, thank you. I won't have you meddle with my body and mind."

"You don't trust me?"

"Frankly, no. I don't know you. I don't know the extend of your powers. You stand here in front of me, looking and talking like a beautiful human woman, which you are not. You tell me about Thomas McClary as if only days have gone by since he lived here, yet it has been a thousand years since the colonists landed on Nu-Eden. That makes you at least two thousand years old."

The Xandra stood in the shadows, her eyes livid green flames against the darkness of her face. "I am much older than that," she said, her voice almost a whisper. "It is true. I am alien to you. You have no idea how alien. Before Humans, there were the Genaar. I learned from them, became like them. Then the Humans came. When I melded with Tom, Anina, and Angela, I adapted, began to think and act like a human. After absorbing the other human colonists I changed even more. You are right, I am not human. I am much more than that." She stepped forward, into the pale light that fell through the window.

Lambert stared at her naked body, at her full, perfect breasts, at the dark triangle below her flat belly. She touched his cheek. "I am more woman than any human woman you have ever met or will ever meet again, John Lambert. I am the fantasy of every man. I am your fantasy come alive. Remember, I looked into your mind. You cannot deny me." She put her arms around him, pulled him to the stony, hard floor.

He moaned, fell between her opening thighs and let her push down his trousers. His manhood had grown hard, and with a deep-throated cry he entered her welcoming softness.

Awareness of his surroundings fell away like a discarded cloak.

Chapter Twenty

Lt. Wang decided to spend the night in one of the tents with Tamsy, the Xandra-born girl. He seemed to be quite taken in by her.

Beringer didn't really care. He had his own problems to deal with. Taking a few deep breaths, he stared at the bright orbs of the two satellites. Somewhere up there circled the alien station. Did Starfinder spend his time watching the huge screen that displayed the image of Nu-Eden? Did he wonder what happened to the small exploration team? Did he care? Beringer really didn't know anything about the alien leader. As a matter of fact, he knew very little about the huge space station.

According to Starfinder, two thousand colonists were sent down to settle on Nu-Eden. Add the fifty men and women Beringer saw. Such a small number of people did not warrant the need for a huge spaceship like that.

Not for the first time Beringer wondered about this. What did the aliens hide in the bowels of the station? What kind of weapons did they possess?

The few devices Starmote displayed gave Beringer enough reason to ponder that question.

Thinking of Starmote made a pulse throb in his groin. She seemed cool and calculating, but he felt strangely attracted to her. He found her beautiful, sensuous, and totally alien. Inhaling the cool, humid air, he became aware again of the pungent exotic fragrance. It seemed to become stronger at night. He didn't wear his nose-filter any longer. Obviously, the particles that clung to the air were not dangerous to Humans, and the filters didn't seem to make much difference.

Pheromones, Starmote had said. That's all they were, some kind of pheromone.

The night was not silent. In the distance he heard the challenging roar of a large beast. Something drummed in the nearby shrubbery, and once he saw what looked like a flock of geese passing in front of one of the moons.

He felt a breeze on his bare arms, and then he heard the whisper of a pair of flapping wings behind him. Whirling around, he drew his laser from its holster, lowered it when he saw the dark, fragile form of a familiar figure.

She folded her wings behind her. Small teeth flashed white in her black face. "I have found you again," she said softly and came closer.

"So you are real," he said, his voice hoarse. In his groin the thumping of his pulse felt like the beating of a second heart. "What do you want from me?"

She laughed, her hand touched his neck. "Last night I sensed your great need and I tried to still it. I have come back to give you the pleasure you crave so much."

Her red glowing eyes seemed to pull him into her, but he fought to keep his senses under control. He managed to let out a short laugh, it sounded like the barking of one of the hounds. "What do *you* crave?" he asked.

"You know," she whispered beside his ear. "I want your blood." She took his hand and pulled him with her. "Come, let us go to a bit more secluded place."

He let her draw him toward one of the ponds. Underneath a wide spreading tree she got to her knees in front of him, opened his belt and pushed down his pants. Taking his already erect member into her small hands, she looked up at him with her glowing eyes, smiled, and then she put her lips on the swollen head of his penis. Her tongue flicked out, began licking him. Even with his foggy mind he registered the forked tip and the unusual length of her tongue.

Her lips opened wider. When she sucked him into her mouth, he felt the prick of her needle fangs as she bit down. Instead of pain he experienced great pleasure. After awhile she freed him and pushed him gently onto his back. With spread, slowly beating wings she straddled him, hovered above him.

Her hand found his penis, guided it toward the dark thick triangle between her slim legs. Her eyes never left his face when she lowered herself with agonizing slowness. Groaning, he lifted his hips off the ground, thrusting deep into her soft orifice.

She laughed, let her weight settle on him and began snapping her pelvis, fast and furious. When his orgasm approached, she stretched out on top of him, pressed her slim, naked body against his. Folding her wings like a dark blanket around them, she put her lips to his neck. The pleasure of his orgasm, when it came, concealed the sting of her needle thin fangs.

She stopped feeding before his over-stimulated pleasure center had a chance to register anything else but pleasure.

Closing his eyes, he lay underneath her light body, aware of her small, soft breasts warm against his skin. For a moment he forgot what she was. For a little while he pretended that she was a young human girl, and not some alien blood-sucking creature. His thoughts were incoherent and confused. He had trouble formulating clear thoughts.

They lay like that for a long time, his penis still hard, lodged inside Naomi's tight vaginal channel. She played with him and let her inner muscles ripple around his organ. When he came inside her with great force, she sank her fangs into his jugular, again

Then she released him.

His mind cleared very fast. Looking at her dark winged form outlined against the sky, he said, "Don't go yet."

"Why not?" she asked, chuckled. "You're still not satisfied?"

Smiling weakly, he sat up, fought a wave of nausea. "I want to talk with   you."
Naomi laughed. "Talk? No human ever talks to a Shadow-Angel."

"I do." He padded the ground beside him. "Come, sit with me. I would like to know more about you."

She slid to the ground, gracefully and silently. Sitting cross-legged in front of him, she spread her black wings, letting them rest on either side of her. "Speak," she said, studying his face.

"Where do you live?" he asked her, his eyes looking at her small, conical breasts. She saw his look and laughed. "Do you really want to know things about me, or do you just want to stare at my body?"

"Both," he said and grinned.

She shook her head. "You are a strange one. Most Humans loathe my kind. They say we are cursed, evil. Given a chance, they kill us without mercy. Why are you different?"

He shrugged. "Humans have been battling discrimination of one kind or another since the dawn of time. Be it the color of skin, the shape of the eyes, or worshipping the wrong god. They are all good reasons to kill a fellow human being. It is part of humanity, part of our heritage. I grew up in a tolerant society, but hatred toward what is different probably still lurks deep inside me." He looked into her face, captivated by her beauty.

Looking into her dark eyes, he noticed the long lashes, saw for the first time the perfection of her black skin. So smooth and without a blemish. "Why would anyone want to kill you?" he asked in a soft whisper.

She seemed suddenly uncomfortable under his scrutiny. "Are you certain you are a human?" she asked.

He chuckled. "What I've seen on this world sometimes makes me wish I weren't."

"You are not from this world?"

"I come from far away, in space and time," he answered, trying to evade the question. "So tell me, where do you live? Are there others like you?"

"I am one of many. We live deep in the forest, where no human can find us."

"Do you live in a village?"

"Like Humans? No, not like Humans. We build our houses high in the trees so we are closer to the sky. We sleep during the day, fly and feed at night"

"What do you do when you don't suck someone's blood or fuck someone?"

She showed her fangs. "What do *you* do when you don't get fucked?" she countered.

"I perform my duties."

"So do I, but most of the time, I live."

"What exactly is it you do? I mean, do you have children? Elderly? Are there any male angels?"

"We have no children, no males and there are no elderly. We always look like this."

"How do you propagate, produce offspring? You say you have no males, yet you copulate. You have breasts, female sex organs. For what purpose?"

She laughed. "We need blood, human blood. We do not kill for it. Copulating with human males is part of our survival. That is the way it is, how it has always been."

"But how do you multiply?"

"We are born fully grown, with all the knowledge we need to survive. The Xandra is our mother." She rose to her feet, shook out her wings. "I hear someone approaching. If you want to know more let us walk into the forest."

He pulled up his pants and draped his shirt over his shoulders. Then he walked beside her on one of the paths that led deeper into the trees. It was darker here. The light from the two moons didn't penetrate the canopy above them. She stopped, leaned against the thick trunk of a tree. He could barely see her in the dark, only her softly glowing eyes.

"The Humans," he said, "where do they live?"

"Some live in houses, like the family who lives here. Some prefer to live in large groups, in villages and towns. Many live in the City with the Mother."

"Are there any other cities, maybe far away from here?"

"There is another city beyond the big lake. The people there call themselves *The_Pure-Ones.* They hate all Xandra-born and those who associate with them. Many men are crossing over into the land of the Mother and are killing Xandra-born and Humans."

"These men, who killed the people on this farmstead, are they members of The Pure-Ones?"

"Yes, they are. But this was only a small group. I saw a large number of them not far from here. I think they want to go the City. A few nights ago, when I drank the blood of one of them, I overheard others. They talked about a Holy War."

Beringer cursed silently. A Holy War!

He had never been a religious man, but he had associated with many who were. Captain Cunningham had been one of them. Sometimes they had discussed religion, and there had been a few friendly arguments. But both men had agreed to one thing: there was nothing more dangerous than a religious fanatic.

"Why do they call it a Holy War?" he asked.

Naomi laughed. "Don't you know? The Xandra-born are all abominations, evil. *Spawn of Satan* they call us. Only True-Humans are good." She stood suddenly very close to him. He smelled her musky, sweet odor. Her breasts grazed his bare skin. Between his legs his penis began to swell. One of her hands moved inside his pants, soft fingers curled around his erection, with the other hand she pushed down his pants.

She was strong. Slowly she forced him to the ground, straddled him. He felt his aching member slide into pure pleasure, as her tight, creamy sex-organ swallowed him up.

While she rode him, the gaze of her glowing eyes held him in their hypnotic spell. He thought of nothing else but the pulsing, soft vice that sent waves of ecstasy throughout his body. He erupted inside her, crushed her to his chest. His hands dug into her pumping small fleshy buttocks. Her black wings shut out the diffused light that managed to penetrate the canopy of the trees to illuminate the path they were lying on. He didn't feel the sting as her needle-fangs sank into his neck, wouldn't have cared if he had.

When reasoning again entered his befuddled mind, she stood above him. A dark, ghostly shadow.

"I could have drained your blood right now," she said softly. "Could have killed you had I chosen so."

"I guess you could have," he said, "why didn't you?"

"Because it is against my nature to kill. Could you kill me?"

Beringer lay there, looking up at her shadowy form. "I probably could, if I had to," he answered slowly.

"Then ask yourself, Human: who really is the evil one?"

She held out a hand, helped him up. A ray of light fell on her face. Her eyes and lips seemed to mock him.

"My name is Beringer," he said. "Les Beringer." His hand touched her cheek. "I could never kill or hurt you."

She smiled, put her lips to his in a fleeting kiss. "I cannot go back with you. There is someone at the pond. It is best I am not seen with you."

"How did you find me?" he asked her as she turned away from him.

"Once I've tasted your blood you are linked to me," she said over her shoulder.

He watched her walk silently deeper into the forest. Her wings trailed behind her like a black cloak. Then he walked slowly back the trail they had come, deep in thought. When Starmote treated the puncture wounds in his neck after his first encounter with the Shadow-Angel, she found traces of a poisonous substance in his blood. It probably wasn't poison, just something that had been injected into his system by Naomi. Something that would transmit his whereabouts to her. A bio-transmitter.

When he came to the pond he heard gentle splashing. Looking across the pond, he saw someone swimming toward the shore where he stood.

"Couldn't sleep?" a female voice called to him. It was Starmote. When she reached the shallow end, she rose out of the water, stood looking at him.

He stared at her naked breasts. They strutted taut and solid from her ribcage, larger and fuller than Naomi's. Her pubic area lay in semi-darkness, but he remembered the small black triangle. The third moon bathed her muscular body with reddish light, creating a beautiful vision, like the incarnation of some alien sex-goddess. He desired her more than ever, even though he had just spent the night in the embrace of another, equally desirable and alien woman.

"The water is refreshing," Starmote said. He kept staring at her, only remotely aware of what she said.

"Are you alright?" she asked.

Shaking his head to clear it, he tore his gaze away from her naked body and looked into the sky. "That's a strange moon," he said hoarsely. "So big and so red." The pulse in his loins pounded hard, he became aware of the strong, familiar fragrance in the air. Looking around, he saw the purple flowers at the edge of the pond.

He took the time to remove his trousers and underwear, folded them neatly and kept them in a little pile beside his shirt. Knowing that Starmote must be aware of his erection, he ran into the water and dove under the dark surface.

Damn! What was wrong with him? He had seen plenty of beautiful women before! None had ever affected him like this.

He surfaced, took a deep breath, looked back toward shore where Starmote still stood, her beautiful body still bathed in the reddish moonlight. She watched him out of dark, curious eyes. Was she affected the same way he was? Did she want him? He didn't know. She had offered herself before.

He could not afford to have a relationship with her, not now, not at this time, not as her superior on this mission.

When this was over…

He turned onto his back, floated in the water, his eyes closed.

His erection had not gone down. He didn't care.

Chapter Twenty-one

John Lambert lay on the soft purple sand and stared dreamily at the rippling water of the lake. Naked girls were frolicking in the small waves among the mass of floating plants that covered about a quarter of the lake.

Virni lay beside him, stroking his back with gentle fingers. "What are you thinking about, John Lambert?" she asked.

He turned his head, looked into large alien eyes. "About this place. About you. Why did you stay?"

She smiled and touched his cheek. "Because of you." She rose gracefully to her feet. "Come, swim with me in the *Water that gives Life.*"

He shook his head. "I don't know how. I've never seen this much water before, not this close. It scares me."

"Virni laughed. "There is nothing to fear. Come, I will be beside you."

"You go ahead." Lambert said. "I'll watch you."

She pulled her mouth into a small pout. "Don't you want to be with me?"

"I do, but I just don't feel like going into the water. And as I said, I can't swim, anyway."

"Alright, but tonight, when the two Sky-Wanderers are in the sky, I will collect your seed, John Lambert." She turned and ran to join the other girls. Lambert watched her round naked buttocks jiggle up and down as she ran gracefully toward the water. Before she jumped in, she turned once to look at him, then she dove into the waves, lost herself among the others. They all looked alike, he could not tell them apart.

Strange, Lambert thought, *how they look so much like the Genaar.* He made a mental note to talk to Commander Beringer about that.

All these naked girls! And all of them beautiful. It was enough to give a young man a constant hard-on. His thoughts drifted back to the previous night. Much of what happened seemed nothing more than a foggy memory, especially the time he spent in the embrace of the woman who called herself The Xandra.

Pleasure. He remembered pleasure.

The Xandra. Who was she? *What* was she?

Why had he not been briefed?

There were just so many questions. He cursed the secrecy that was so much a part of the military. Everything was *need-to-know*. It might have been to his advantage to know a little more about the situation on this planet.

He blinked against the alien sun in the cloudless sky. For the first time in his life he had no artificial barrier between himself and a hot burning star. The rays were warm on his bare skin. He wondered if the radiation would harm him. He decided to put on his shirt and take a stroll through the small settlement.

"There you are," said a female voice behind him, just as he reached for his shirt. He turned and looked at the dark-haired woman, Mirtin. He even remembered her name.

"What is this place?" she asked.

Lambert shrugged. "The woman I spoke to last night called it her *Sanctuary*. It is peaceful here."

Mirtin sighed. "This is the first time since we've come to this cursed place that I feel somewhat secure. You have no idea what we've been through." She looked at him with a thoughtful expression. Then she crouched down beside him. "That rig you're flying, it looks like an antique model. I don't remember ever seeing one that old. Tell me, what planetary system are you from?"

Lambert sat up. His brows knotted together when he stared at her. "Well," he said, "I gather this means you are not a native to this world."

"I'm not, and neither are you, that much is obvious. What are you doing here? Where is your Dive-ship? Are you with a military unit? Are you possibly a member of an outlawed group?"

"Many questions!" Lambert said thoughtfully. "I can't answer you until you answer some of mine. Do *you* belong to a military outfit?"

"Yes and no. I am here on a rescue mission. Things went wrong. That is all I will tell you." She stood up and began to unbutton her shirt. "I'm going for a swim. I feel grimy and dirty." She threw her shirt to the ground and stepped out of her pants.

Lambert stared at the thick black triangle below her flat belly, and then at her large full breasts. Her gray, slightly slanted eyes stared back at him defiantly for a moment. "What about you?" she asked. "Does your religion forbid you to go swimming in the nude?"

He grinned, slightly embarrassed. "The water scares me. I am used to enclosed systems. A small pool is what I prefer."

Shaking her head, she walked slowly toward the lake. His eyes were glued to her voluptuous body, watched the play of her fleshy, but solid buttocks. She put her toes into the water to test it. Then she waded in and finally dove into an incoming wave.

Another beautiful woman, he thought, *a human woman.* She was tall, as tall as he was. Even with her close-cropped hair she looked attractive. A sudden realization struck him. This woman was from the present, his future. He came from her past.

Suddenly he found himself a stranger in an unfamiliar world, the world he had known long gone. A thousand years gone.

She was as alien to him as Virni was. He had to find out more about the world she lived in, needed to know what happened to Earth, and to Ganymede, his place of birth.

Mirtin came running out of the water, laughing. Brushing herself dry with her hands, she stood in front of him. Again, he admired the soft curves of her body, her long, slim legs, the way her full breasts stood high on her ribcage. The cool water made her nipples rigid and the wind created goose-bumps on her satiny skin.

She became suddenly conscious of his staring and turned away from him. Her buttocks were round and firm, he felt himself responding to her.

"Are you comparing my body to that of the woman who took you away when we arrived?" Mirtin asked while pulling up her baggy pants. "Who was she, anyway?"

"She calls herself The Xandra, *the Mother of Light*," Lambert said.

"The Mother of Light?" Mirtin mused. "Viran talked about her. She's supposed to be some kind of goddess. What do you know about her?"

"I have no idea what she is," Lambert admitted. "My superior never briefed me. I wasn't even supposed to leave the shuttle. However, here I am, lying on an alien beach, talking to a beautiful, possibly alien, woman." He rose to his feet and put on his shirt. Looking at Mirtin, he said, "I have comrades somewhere out there who might need my help. If they tried to get in touch with me they couldn't, because I deserted my post. I must get back to my shuttle, or the Commander will have my hide."

"The Commander, eh?" said Mirtin. "So you are a member of a military unit. Who authorized your landing on this planet?"

Lambert stopped walking, gave the woman a long look. "Listen," he said after some hesitation. "Maybe it's time for some explanations. I don't know if I should trust you, but what-the-hell. You seem to be stranded here, you are more or less at my mercy, or so it seems. I think it may be to our mutual benefit if we exchange information."

She nodded in agreement. "Let's go and sit in the shade of that big tree over there," she said.

The found a bench made from stone, barely visible in the knee-high grass. Lambert felt almost guilty when his boots crushed the purple flowers that grew everywhere. Inhaling the sweet fragrance produced an almost intoxicating feeling and he became sexually aroused. Beside him, Mirtin's breathing seemed to have increased. She wiped her forehead and gave him a sidelong glance.

"I feel a little strange," she said, breathlessly, and began to unbutton her shirt.

Lambert watched her naked breasts tumble out. Then she pushed down her pants and began tugging on his. "I need you," she whispered and freed his already stiff member.

He fell on top of her, her legs spread wide and then he slipped inside her. Crying out, she wrapped her long legs around his torso and raked his back with sharp fingernails. Shuddering, he emptied himself into her soft sheath, but she refused to let him go. "Not yet," she pleaded with a sobbing voice, "not yet."

Still hard, he moved with a steady rhythm between her clutching thighs. *A thousand years is a long time*, he thought.

When they finally broke apart, she lay beside him, trying to catch her breath.

"That was the first time I got raped," Lambert chuckled.

She slapped his shoulder. "You wanted it as badly as I," she said. "What exactly happened here?"

"I think it's these flowers." Lambert crushed one between his fingers, inhaled. A gentle fluttering in his loins confirmed his suspicion.

"Some kind of aphrodisiac," Mirtin said. She looked over the sea of purple blooms. "There is a great opportunity for making a lot of money here. This planet could be turned into a resort for the ultimate pleasure seekers."

Lambert sat up. "I suppose, but it might meet with some opposition from the locals." He watched a butterfly land on one of the flowers, scooped it up with his hands. When he opened his hands, it didn't fly away, just sat there, its small colorful wings moving slowly. "This is one of the few insects I've seen on this planet," he observed. "I wonder what purpose it serves."

"It flitters from flower to flower and helps to propagate the plants, I guess," Mirtin said. "Usually that is how it works."

"Usually. Here too?"

"I don't know. I haven't studied the local plant life."

"What have you studied?"

Mirtin shrugged. "Not much so far. Since we set foot on this planet we've experienced one mishap after another. This is the best time I have had yet." She leaned over and kissed him softly on the lips. Then she looked at him, "Don't take this personally," she said. "What we just did doesn't really mean anything." She gave a little laugh. "We haven't become lovers. We fucked, that's all."

"That defines it, I guess." Lambert got to his feet. "And here I was beginning to think we had something going." He smiled and held out a hand. She took it and pulled herself up. When she stood in front of him, her naked breasts brushed against his bare chest. She looked down, saw his erection, and smiled. "I should be flattered," she commented, "but I know it is not me. Come, let's get away from these flowers before we do something neither one of us really wants to do."

They didn't even bother getting dressed, just picked up their clothing and ran out of the small meadow. Both of them were panting when they reached the narrow tiled walkway that led to the small cluster of houses and huts.

Someone came walking toward them. Lambert recognized the blond girl, Vienne.

"I was looking for you," Vienne said as she came closer. She narrowed her eyes, shook her head and said with an accusing voice, "Do you have to fuck every male you come across?"

Mirtin lifted her shoulder, buttoned up her shirt. Then she looked at Lambert. "Do me a favor, walk with her to that bench and sit there for awhile with her."

"I don't want to sit on any bench," Vienne said sharply.

"Humor me, Vienne," Mirtin said, "please."

"Are you sure?" Lambert said, hesitatingly.

"I am, just go."

Reluctantly Vienne walked into the field with Lambert. Mirtin watched them and smiled when Vienne suddenly stopped.

"Something strange is happening," she heard the blond girl say. Vienne's hand went to her shirt, unbuttoned it. Mirtin saw Lambert stare at Vienne's small exposed breasts. He looked up when he heard

Mirtin laugh and call, "Bring her back." Grabbing Vienne's hand, he pulled her with him as he ran out of the meadow.

"You're a bitch," Vienne cursed Mirtin, "what's happened to me?" She kept rubbing her breasts.

Lambert stood, breathing heavily, beside the blond girl. "You *are* a bitch," he growled, looking at Mirtin, his face flushed. She could see the erection in his pants.

"Experience is the best teacher," she said to Vienne. "I should have let him fuck you." She turned away, began walking toward the houses.

Lambert grinned at Vienne, leered at her still exposed breasts. "She's right," he said. "I think I would have enjoyed it."

Vienne closed her shirt angrily. "I hate this planet, and I hate you."

"Why would you hate me?" Lambert asked, perplexed. "I'm the guy who rescued you, remember? You could show a little gratitude."

"I am grateful, but that doesn't mean I have to fuck you!" Vienne glared at him, blue eyes blazing. When she saw his hurt look her face softened. "I'm sorry," she said, "I don't really hate you, in particular. I don't even know you. It's just… this place is driving me crazy. I was never prepared for this."

"She doesn't like any men, just so you know," Mirtin called over her shoulder.

"Oh," Lambert said. He looked at Vienne. "I remember now, the Xandra told me. It didn't really register. What a shame, such beauty, wasted." He walked beside the blond girl. "It's the flowers," he said to her. "Whatever you felt back there, it wasn't your or my doing. It's those damn flowers."

Vienne stayed silent, just walked, looking down at the tiled ground.

"Nothing happened," she said after awhile. "Forget it."

They were walking past the first house. A man and a woman were picking weeds out of a flower bed. The woman looked up, waived to them. "Lovely day," she called and wiped a strand of hair out of her eyes.

She was beautiful, of undetermined age. She smiled at Lambert. "I saw you in the field of the *Flowers of Love.* I was tempted to join you. We usually don't go into the field until night, when the fragrance of the blossoms becomes much stronger."

Lambert smiled back at her. "We are strangers here," he said, "we are not used to your customs. I hope we didn't offend anyone."

The woman laughed. "How can you offend anyone when you perform the act of love? The Mother teaches us that anytime is time for love. We are allowed to make love without collecting a man's seeds for the Mother."

"Well, that is good to know," Lambert said. "We don't want to break any laws."

Smiling, the woman walked toward them. She stopped in front of Lambert, looked into his face. He noticed her soft, smooth skin, the deep green color of her eyes. "I am Tara. I am a daughter of the Xandra," she said and touched his cheek. "You are a True-Human. I would be honored to collect your seed tonight."

Lambert felt the blood rushing into his face. Embarrassed by the woman's open invitation, he feigned ignorance. "As I said, I am a stranger and not familiar with your ways. I don't quite understand the meaning of your words."

She laughed and fingered the necklace of precious stones he wore around his neck. "A gift from one of the Nymphs, am I right? So you cannot be as ignorant as you claim, but I'd be happy to show you more of our ways, tonight by the pond."

Lambert glared at Vienne who snorted disgustedly. "I suppose you know what she's talking about?"

The blond girl chuckled without humor. "She wants to fuck you, maybe you understand that!" she said and shook her head. "It seems that everything turns around sex on this crazy planet. Women are nothing but pleasure-objects, seed-collectors for an imaginary goddess, this… this sentient plant they call *The Mother*."

"You speak like the *Unbelievers*," the woman said. "The Mother is real, she gave me life, and I collect a man's seeds for her so she can make new life." She looked at Vienne's slim body. "You are a True-Human. You create life inside your belly. I cannot do that."

"Why not?" Vienne asked, defiance in her voice. "You can fuck with a man!"

Smiling, Tara shook her head. "You speak of the act with disgust. I fail to understand. Coupling with a man brings pleasure to both of us, it is a good thing. The Xandra gave us that gift. All she asks from us is to collect the seeds for her."

Vienne's blue eyes studied the Xandra-born. "You look and act like a woman," she said with a low voice, "but, obviously, you are not even human."

Tara looked into Vienne's eyes. "I am born of the Xandra," she said proudly. "I may not be Woman-born--yet, I have as much right to live as any True-Human."

"I never disputed your right to live," Vienne retorted.

"You are so angry. Why?"

"I don't know." Vienne brushed her hair with a violent gesture. "I haven't been myself ever since I came here. There are feelings inside me that I never had before. "She gave a sudden laugh, and burst out, "I long for the embrace of that savage, who calls himself Viran, figure that one out."

A low chuckle from Mirtin made Vienne look at her companion. "What?" she demanded.

Mirtin lifted her hands. "I didn't say a thing."

"Viran?" Lambert said. "Wasn't that the man I brought here?'

"The same one," Mirtin nodded. "I told you, we are his friends."

"More than that, it seems," Lambert remarked dryly. "By the way, I wonder what happened to him."

Chapter Twenty-two

He opened his eyes. Above him he saw Rah and Roh, the two Sky-wanderers, two bright, yellow disks in a purple sky. It surprised him to see them. Sitting up he found himself surrounded by water. There were shapes splashing all around him, female shapes. Young girls, their wet long black hair plastered to their skulls, their bare breasts jiggling as they frolicked in the water. He heard their silvery laughs.

Water-Nymphs. Looking around, he noticed that he sat on a carpet of thick purple petals in the middle of a giant plant. Memory flooded back painfully.

The black heavy head of his own war-hammer blotted out the sky; dull pain shot through his body as the hammer smashed into his face. His hands went to his chest. He remembered being hit by something with great force. When he looked down at himself, he saw only smooth, bronzed skin. Sensing movement behind him, he turned and saw a woman kneeling in the center of the plant. He recognized her.

"Greetings, Viran," she said and smiled. Shaking her long red hair out of her beautiful face she reached out and touched him. Her touch felt like the sting of a *Fire-Frog*, but instead of pain it brought pleasure,

"How did I get here?" he asked.

Her hand moved up to his face, stroked his temple. "I almost lost you, my Champion," she said, her eyes seemed concerned.

"How did I get here?" he asked again. His eyes widened, he stared at her. "Am I dead?"

She laughed, bent forward and kissed him. Then she stood up. Her long hair fell, covered her like a red veil, but he could still see the outlines of her body. "Not dead," she said. "You are very much alive."

He rose to his feet, towered over her. "Am I one of your creatures?" he asked with a harsh voice.

Again she laughed, stepped up to him. Her naked breasts touched his chest. "No, and you will never be one of my creatures. You would be useless to me. I need you as you are. A True-Human."

"I don't understand. How can I be alive? I was killed."

"Almost, and you would have died had I not been inside you."

"How?" He felt himself responding to her touch, took a step backwards. He needed answers, not sex.

"Remember, when you were with me, I told you that I would be part of you forever? It was true. I put a little bit of myself inside your head, just enough to keep track of you." Her hand reached out again, she put a finger against his lips. "Don't get angry," she said. "When a man lies with me he must pay a price. I gave you pleasure beyond anything you can imagine. It is a small price. There was a reason. I have great plans for you."

"How about my own plans?" He said angrily. "I have plans, too. You can't control me!"

"I have no such intentions. What I tell you now may not please you, but it was the only way. When I had you brought to me you were near death, your backbone shattered, half your face and skull caved in, and part of your brain destroyed. I had to do a lot of repairs." Her hands stroked his chest. She looked into his eyes and smiled. "I had to rebuild and replace much of your brain matter. I used parts of myself. Pieces of your lung, your backbone, ribs, all had to be replaced. You and I are linked closer together than any True-Human has ever been linked to me. I have given you abilities and powers that no Human ever possessed. Let me show you."

He almost cried out with joy when he felt her mental touch.

We are one, she said inside his head. *Yet we are also apart. Wherever you are you will be able to communicate with me. All the knowledge I possess will be yours when you need it.*

She withdrew. "There is something else I want to show you," she spoke aloud. He heard the flutter of wings above him and looked up. A winged figure glided down from the treetops, landed beside Viran on the Xandra-plant.

"Hello, Viran," she said, standing wide-legged in front of him.

"Angela!" He stared at her belly. His gaze moved down to the junction between her legs. Where once had been smooth skin he saw a swollen, split mound, covered with blond curls.

She smiled at him. "The Mother gave me what I wanted," she said and stepped closer. She looked him in the eyes, her fingers curled around his penis. "You'll be the first," she whispered, "Come."

He looked for the Xandra, but she had disappeared.

"We are alone, Viran," Angela said huskily. Her hands were on his chest, pushed gently, but forcefully. He sank down, lay back on the soft thick carpet of petals. Spreading her great wings wide, Angela mounted him. He felt himself slide into her soft channel. Her eyes closed for a moment as she hovered above him, only the inner muscles of her new organ fluttered around his rigid penis.

"It is more beautiful than I imagined," she whispered. Her blue eyes opened, looked into his. Then she began to rotate her lower body. He groaned as the waves of pleasure began and stared at her beautifully shaped breasts. They seemed larger than he remembered. Her whole body looked fuller, bigger, more muscular.

She saw him scrutinize her, laughed and snapped her pelvis back and forth with furious speed. "I was dead," she said, "but the Mother created this new body for me."

"You are not Angela, not really!" Viran said and called out as a powerful climax gripped him.

"I am Angela. I have all her memories, but this body is better, stronger. I am not the frail creature I used to be."

She closed her eyes again, clamped down hard as her first orgasm raced through her body. He felt the warm liquid of her discharge and dug his strong fingers into her hips. She rode him for a long time. Then she released him, knelt on all fours and insisted he enter her that way. Getting behind her, he ran his hand over her white round buttocks. The puffed lips of her vagina beckoned below them. Spreading her thighs with one hand, he guided his penis into the pink crevice, slid deep into her. She arched her back, pushed up her posterior. Her spread wings rested on either side of her. Clasping his hands around her narrow waist, he began pumping, his eyes glued to the spot where they were joined together. When the first rays of the sun fell through the treetops she was still not satisfied.

"Don't stop!" she cried as he moved untiring on top of her between her widespread thighs, "don't ever stop."

He shuddered as he emptied himself into her again, pulled out and knelt between her spread legs. "The Mother may not have done you a great favor by giving you what you craved," Viran said.

She clamped her knees around his hips. "This was the first time for me, Viran," she said with pouting lips. "Don't give up so soon. Just one more time, please."

He smiled. "Just one more time," he said and moved forward. His penis became hard as he touched its tip to her swollen labia. She sighed when he entered her, dug her fingers into his muscular chest. As his organ moved in and out of her, he thought he heard silent laughter inside his head, but so faint that it may have been only his imagination.

Chapter Twenty-three

He didn't recognize her at first. She wore a short skirt made entirely from purple flowers. A ring of flowers wound themselves around her breasts, leaving only her long, dark nipples uncovered. Small white flowers were braided into her luxurious black hair.

"Virni," he said, his voice catching in his throat.

"John Lambert," she smiled, looking as beautiful as a vision out of a dream.

He smelled the heady fragrance of the flowers, felt his body react to the onslaught of pheromones. Above him in the sky the two alien satellites threw double shadows in front of the girl, as she walked toward him.

"The Mother instructed me to collect your seed tonight," she said softly when she stood in front of him. Her large purple eyes seemed to glow with a soft fire as she stared into his.

He reached out to crush her to him, to throw her into the soft sand, to plunge his erect penis into her alien vagina. She laughed, evaded his grasp. Then she took his hand. "Not here, John Lambert. A special place has been chosen. Come."

He followed her, like a ram that has been chosen for slaughter, blinded by lust, but not knowing what waited for him. She led him down a narrow path, into a small glade. He saw a pond, in its middle floated a giant purple flower, surrounded by a mass of thick green leaves. A group of girls knelt inside the pond; nude bodies gleamed in the light of the two moons, all of them looked like Virni.

They formed a circle. Virni pulled Lambert inside. She lay down on the soft ground, pulled her flower skirt past her hips and spread her legs. One of the girls knelt beside her, covered her genitals with a thin transparent sheet. It flowed across her belly, inner thighs, and then into her vagina.

Lambert saw all this with detached curiosity, barely aware of the two girls who pulled down his pants. His freed penis strutted, solid and hard. He did not need any encouragement. With a loud sob, he fell between Virni's widespread thighs. Stabbing frantically, he managed to slide his stiff pole into her soft creamy sheath. He didn't notice the guiding hand of one of the other nymphs.

Great waves of pure pleasure washed through his body. When Virni offered one of her nipples, he took it eagerly into his mouth, drank from her sweet nectar. Strength and stamina flowed into every fiber of his body. Without tiring he moved between the alien girl's clutching thighs. Roaring, he finally emptied his precious load into her vessel.

Two of the nymphs pulled him gently up and pushed him over into the embrace of another one. Unaware that it wasn't Virni anymore who writhed underneath him, he rocked on top of her soft body. They all looked alike, behaved alike. After filling another seed pouch, they made him lie on his back He watched one of the girls hover over his erect penis. Seeing and feeling it glide into her smooth belly, he cried out when the pleasure overwhelmed him.

They finally let him rest. He lay in the soft grass. They took turns kissing him, letting their saliva drip into his mouth. He sucked on their breasts and feasted on the sweet honey they offered.

Then they mounted him again, drained his spurting organ and made him call out until he was hoarse. The third moon hung high in the sky, when Lambert found himself alone with Virni. Lying in his arms, she stroked his chest, kissed him gently on the lips. "The Mother is pleased," she said, "you have filled many seed pouches."

The fog that enveloped Lambert's brain for the last few hours disappeared. His memory of the night patchy, he remembered little, except for flashes of undulating naked bodies, bare breasts hovering in front of his face, the taste of sweet nectar from nipples thrust into his mouth.

"How many girls did I have sex with?" he asked.

Virni laughed softly, kissed him gently. "Many, what does it matter?"

"It matters to me. Does it not bother you? Aren't you jealous?"

"They are my sisters. We are happy and honored to serve the Mother. Why should I be jealous?"

He searched her face. "Do you love me?"

She smiled, touched his cheek. "Yes, John Lambert, I love you."

He sat up, looked at the pond, at the giant flower floating on the dark water. A sudden silent laughter inside his head.

Then he saw *Her*.

She stood inside the flower. The light from the moon bathed her naked body with a red glow. Her long hair framed her face and upper body like a curtain of fire. "You have done well, John Lambert," said a ghostly voice inside him. "You did not disappoint me."

When he looked closer, he saw only the empty plant.

He wiped his forehead. *I'm beginning to hallucinate*, he thought and looked at Virni. "Did you see her?" he asked.

Virni nodded and laughed. "The Mother, she loves you, too," she said and sat up to kiss him.

Lambert shook his head. "I don't know what to believe. You tell me that you love me, your sisters love me, the so-called Mother loves me. All this love, the unbelievable sex. It doesn't quite fit. That mortally wounded barbarian we brought here, and those two women I rescued from an uncertain fate. It suggests evil and violence. Not everything is love and happiness on this world."

Virni became silent, and then she smiled sadly. "You are right," she said. "Not everyone shares our happiness." She looked him in the eyes. "You are a True-Human, John Lambert, but you are different. There are those True-Humans who would not couple with me, because I am of the *Xandra*. I don't look human, like the *Others*. But even they are hated and killed by the True-Humans."

"Why is that?"

Virni shrugged. "I don't know. Because we are different, perhaps. They call us *Water-nymphs*."

"Why?"

She lifted her shoulders, again. Lambert studied her face, found it so beautiful, even though she looked so different, alien. How could anyone want to hurt such a lovely and gentle creature? He pulled her into the grass. "Tell me about yourself, Virni," he said. "Where do you live?"

"I live with my sisters by one of the ponds in the forest, but you asked me that already."

"My memory is not the greatest these days. I seem to confuse reality with illusion. What do you do all day?"

She laughed, let her slim fingers trail down his chest. "We spend much time in the water, searching for colored stones and shells. We make beautiful things with our hands."

"Who teaches you?"

"We know much when we leave the pod that nourishes us until we are fully grown. Our older sisters and the Mother teach us more."

"What do you eat?"

"Fruit from the trees, tubers from the ground, fungus that grows everywhere in the forest."

"No meat?"

She shook her head vehemently. "We don't kill other creatures. That is wrong."

"It all sounds so peaceful." Lambert stroked her hair, looked into the depth of her large, alien black eyes. Again he puzzled over the similarity between her and the Genaar females. On the station they had not been allowed to get too close to them. He had never really known one, except for Starmote; and she was very different.

Thinking of Starmote, he became suddenly aware that he had been neglecting his duties. Commander Beringer would not be very pleased if he found out what he did doing these last few days. He had to get back to the Lander. What if the Commander tried to contact him? What if the team came back and found the Lander gone?

He stood up, startling Virni. "What is it?" she asked.

"I have a job, Virni," he said. "Others may depend on me. I have to get back to my ship."

She rose, pressed her naked body against his. Inhaling her fragrance, he felt the blood rushing to his groin. She giggled when his erect penis touched her belly. "More seeds?" she whispered.

"No!" He pushed her away, fighting the urge.

"You don't love me?" Her eyes seemed hurt.

"I do love you," he said, hoarsely, "but I cannot spend my time having sex with you and your sisters. I have a duty to perform. I am sorry."

A breeze from the pond ruffled the large purple petals of the great plant, impregnating the air with its strong and heady fragrance. He put his hands against his temples. "I must get away," he murmured, "I must."

He stumbled down a path. He didn't know if Virni followed him, he didn't care. Darkness seemed to close in around him, the high-pitched scream of a night-creature made him falter. He heard murmuring voices, soft cries. Coming out in a small glade he saw another pond, larger than the one he came from. Figures moved under a tree, more in the water.

"John Lambert," a woman's voice called to him. One of the figures came running toward him. She stopped and laughed happily. "Are there any seeds left inside you?" she asked with a breathless voice.

Tara, the woman from the village, naked and beautiful.

"I never told you my name," he said.

She laughed again, stepped closer. Her green eyes were shaded by her long, dark lashes. "Your friends told me."

"My friends?"

"Yes, Mirtin and Vienne. They are over there." She pointed toward one of the trees.

Lambert stared. He only saw Vienne. There was no mistaking her blond head and her thin, naked body. Her narrow hips snapped furiously back and forth on top of someone hidden in the grass.

"Well, well," he murmured. "That is interesting."

"And there is Mirtin." Tara said.

Mirtin knelt in front of a naked man, her back arched. He moved his hips with lazy precision back and forth. Mirtin's moans and soft cries of pleasure were clearly audible.

"Who are those men?" Lambert asked.

"The one with your blond friend is Torra and the other one is Vork."

"Are they collecting seeds for the Xandra from those men?"

"No, Torra and Vork are Xandra-born. They are not fertile. Their sperm-sacs carry no seeds."

"So why are they doing what they are doing?"

"Pleasure." Tara laughed. "Xandra-born men are in great demand with some True-women. They are great pleasure-givers." She put her hand on his erect penis. "I can give you much pleasure. You are a True-Human. You have seeds that the Mother needs. Let me collect them."

She kissed him hungrily, while her hand stroked his penis. He groaned and let her pull him toward the pond. "I have to get a seed-pouch," she whispered into his ear.

He watched her running into the water, her round and plump buttocks moving gently below her narrow waist. She fished something out of the water, put it between her legs and came back, running, her large breasts bobbing. Smiling, she pushed him onto his back and straddled him.

"There is no hurry," she said, gasped as she impaled herself deeply on his pole. Then she began milking him with great expertise. "Am I giving you as much pleasure as Virni?" she asked.

He lunged upwards, dug his fingers into her gyrating hips.

She acted different from Virni and her nymph-sisters. They had been silent during the act, not so Tara. She gasped and moaned loudly, cried out when she experienced an orgasm.

When she stretched out on top of him her lower body never stopped moving. Taking one of her nipples into his mouth, he began sucking and swallowed the sweet nectar that flowed into his mouth.

Her gift provided him with strength. His arms went around her upper body, he rolled her over, came to rest on top of her. Her legs flew wide open and he moved between them with renewed vigor.

When he came it was with tremendous force. Calling out hoarsely, he emptied his fluid into her sucking canal, filled the seed-pouch with life-giving sperms.

He pulled out, rolled onto his back, his penis still stiff.

Tara got up and went back into the water, where she removed the full seed-pouch from her belly.

A shadow fell over Lambert. He looked up to stare at the nude figure of a winged girl. "You are the one who helped Viran," she said with a sweet clear voice.

Lambert squinted at her. "Are you the same girl who came with him? I thought you were dead."

She laughed. "I am Angela and I was dead, but the Mother brought me back to life." Spreading her great wings, she blotted out the red moon. Then she moved to stand wide-legged above him.

Lambert stared at her beautifully shaped breasts and at the puffy mound of her femininity. Slowly she sank down, her wings moving gently, like a white cloak in a breeze. She took him into her, made him groan when her tight sheath squeezed him gently.

"I am the only one of my kind who can experience the coupling with a man," she said and let her wings lift her up.

"I don't think I have any seeds left inside me," Lambert gasped.

Angela smiled. "It doesn't matter. I'm not collecting your seeds. I do this for myself." Folding her wings behind her, she let her full weight rest in his lap. She closed her eyes and began to rotate her pelvis slowly and lazily. Her inner muscles grabbed his shaft like a soft vice, milked it with a powerful grip.

His eyes were glued to her breasts. They were round and firm, with short, thick nipples. She gasped. Her blue eyes flew open and locked with his. "Come now!" she cried out. "I want to feel you explode inside me."

He didn't need any encouragement. The soft pressure of her vibrating vagina proved too much for him to hold back any longer. He let go and doused her insides with his hot liquid.

She clamped down hard, held him in a tight grip until she had drained him. Sighing, she lifted up and stood staring down at him. "My craving has been satisfied, for the moment," she said softly, "but I don't know for how long. Viran told me that the gift I received may not be so great. I think he is wrong." She spread her wings, rising into the air.

Lambert watched her soar above the treetops, a shadow against the moon for a fleeting moment, before she disappeared.

"I've never seen an Angel who can take a man inside her," said a soft voice beside him."

Lambert looked at Tara. She lay beside him, on her belly. He hadn't heard her come. "How long have you been lying there?" he asked.

She chuckled softly. "Long enough to see your big seed-spitter disappear inside the Angel's belly."

"Why is that so unusual?"

She shrugged. "Only the Shadow-Angels are capable of coupling with a man. But they don't do it for pleasure. This is very strange."

"Her name is Angela."

"Most of them are called that."

"Who are these Shadow-Angels?"

"You don't want to meet one." Tara said seriously. "They may give you great pleasure, but as payment they want your soul."

"So it is as I told Virni already. There exists more than pure love and peace here." Lambert looked to where Vienne had been churning on top of one of the Xandra-men. *He* didn't see her, but then he spied her blond head in the water. The other girl, Mirtin, seemed also gone from under the tree. "This activity takes place every night?" he asked Tara.

She shook her head. "Not every night. Only when all three moons meet in the sky do we celebrate the creation of Life." She smiled and touched his penis. "But we do couple whenever we want to, even without collecting seeds."

"I think I've donated enough seeds already tonight," Lambert said. "I am dry."

Tara laughed. "You could suck on my breasts. My nectar is sweet and will give you strength."

Lambert put his hand on one of her breasts and chuckled. "Your offer is tempting. A man could be quite happy here. All the women are beautiful and willing, a man's paradise, but I think there is more to this place than what is seen on the surface. I can't get the man I shot out of my mind, and his companions didn't act very friendly. Then there is Viran. I found him wounded and bleeding. They shot the winged girl,

Angela, and did who knows what to Mirtin and Vienne. This is not a peaceful world."

He stood up, looked down at himself, realized that he was still naked. "I left my clothing back by the other pond."

When he looked around for the path from which he had come, he saw a slim female figure standing by the edge of the glade. She saw him look, started walking toward him. She carried something in her hands.

"Virni?" he asked.

"I brought your clothing," she said. "You may want to put them back on."

He looked at her, standing there before him, lovely and forlorn. Suddenly he felt guilty. "I'm sorry I ran away like that." He touched her cheek, his gaze wandered to Tara, then back to Virni. "I am usually not like this, I mean, I don't usually jump every woman who offers herself."

Virni put her arms around his neck. "I love you, John Lambert," she whispered. "I've never loved a man before. This is a new feeling for me, but the Mother says it is alright, there is nothing wrong with me."

Lambert smiled sadly. "You and I are of two different species. We live in two different worlds. It would never work."

She kissed him. Then she took his hand. "Come, I will take you to your flying house."

They walked in silence. The red moon had disappeared behind the mountain ridge, leaving darkness behind. Soon the sun would rise and bring a new day to the valley.

Sanctuary.

He found peace here, and love.

Lambert looked up into the alien sky, at the unfamiliar constellations. He realized that his whole world had changed. Nothing would be the same ever again.

Chapter Twenty-four

Viran squatted to look at his reflection in the clear water. He didn't look any different, his eyes were still dark gray-blue, his hair a thick black mane curling down to his shoulders. He didn't feel any different, and yet, his thoughts seemed clearer somehow, and quicker. When he looked at a tree, he became aware of the life-giving fluid rushing up the trunk, into the branches and the leaves. When he listened, he could almost hear the song of life dancing from one tree to another.

Touching the water with one hand, he sensed a gentle vibration flowing through his body. He stood up, stretched and flexed his great muscles.

It felt good to be alive.

Soft footsteps in the grass behind him made him turn around. She looked different, but he knew it was *Her*. A gentle smile played around her full lips. Her thoughts reached out toward him and touched him. *Viran*, she said, *I knew I'd find you here.*

He laughed. "Of course you did," he answered. "Just as I knew you'd come."

Her green eyes sparkled as she looked up at him. "You have adjusted well," she said aloud and brushed a strand of red hair out of her face.

Studying her face, Viran said, "You are the Xandra, yet, you are not tethered to your body."

"No, but I cannot travel freely, like you. I must stay in the Sanctuary to keep my true identity. From time to time I join with the mother-plant to regenerate."

"You are clothed," he observed.

She laughed, smoothed out the wrinkles in her white gown. "A custom I picked up from the Humans. I can remove it if you prefer me naked."

"No, it suits you. I have never seen a female dressed in such finery. The women in my tribe wear rough clothing that hides their soft curves." He touched her cheek with one large hand. "How can I ever love another woman after you?"

Again she laughed and kissed the inside of his palm. "You will, Viran, you will. But I am always with you."

"You said you put part of yourself into me."

"I told you I did. I also told you that I gave you abilities no other man possesses. You were always strong, but now you are stronger. I gave you clarity of thinking. I gave you knowledge which you never had before. You and I will always be connected, but I also created limits to this connection. Had I not done so, you would have lost your human identity."

"How can I still be a True-Human with part of you inside me?"

"But you are, Viran. The human species has great potential. Humans have not yet learned to use many of their abilities. I only enhanced what you already had, you are more than human."

Viran shook his head, looked down at his clenched fist. "I don't feel any different."

"Because you've accepted your natural abilities."

"You say you've put limits on our connection."

The Xandra nodded. "Tell me, when you look at me, what do you see?"

"A beautiful woman," Viran smiled, and added, "A very desirable, beautiful woman."

She stared directly into the bright sun that glared in the blue sky. "You see a human," she said and turned away from him. "I am not human, except when I am in this guise. You and I are completely alien to each other. If I let your mind totally blend with mine you would go insane. I am unique. For millennia I existed alone. Alone and bored. The Humans, and the Genaar before them, have brought me a wealth of knowledge that I never knew existed. I was eager to absorb all these new experiences they brought me, too eager. I made mistakes, but I evolved. There are many concepts I have learned, things like love and hate, good and evil, pleasure and pain. At first it amused me. I looked upon it as playing a game. But there were other things I learned. I learned about violence. I learned about death. Much has changed since the Humans came. I had fun creating different forms of life. But the Humans are murdering my creatures. Until now I have tolerated it, accepted it as a game Humans like to play. It is time for another change. I cannot tolerate this slaughter any longer. I *will* not tolerate it any longer."

She turned around to face him. Her eyes seemed to glow softly. She smiled. She took his hand and led him toward the water. "What do you see?" she asked him.

He looked at the still water of the pond, saw the sleeping plant. A mass of seed-pods the size of his fist floated all around the giant plant.

One swam close to shore. When he bent to lift it out of the water, the Xandra cautioned, "Be careful not to break the lifeline."

A tiny thread trailed from the small pod into the water.

"You are holding your son in your hand," she said. "One of many sons."

Viran stared at the scaly surface of the seed-pouch. ""My son?" he asked, sudden understanding dawning on him.

The Xandra made a sweeping gesture. "There are exactly one hundred seed-pouches; each one holds a human embryo that will grow into your likeness."

She took the pod from his hands, lowered it carefully back into the water. Then she stood up and put her slim arms around his neck. "When you lay in my embrace at the abandoned temple I collected your seed. I chose one hundred of the strongest and transferred them into seed-pouches, which I had then transported here. This is Sanctuary; no harm will come to them in this place."

"How do you know they will all be like me?"

"Because I will it so. I decide what each seed-pouch carries."

"Each seed-pouch? But there must be countless ones!"

She laughed softly. "Not countless. I am aware of each and everyone. I am the Mother."

Viran shook his head in wonder. "You are truly a goddess. I feel humble in your presence."

"Not you, my Viran. You are my Chosen One."

She stepped away from him then. Her slim fingers untied the cord that held her gown together, opened it and let lit slip from her shoulders. Naked, she stood in front of him, a beautiful human woman with a voluptuous inviting body, her breasts firm and solid on her ribcage, the long nipples surrounded by a dark areola. Below her flat belly, red curly hair covered her mound of femininity.

Opening her arms, she smiled at him. "Come, make love to me, Viran. In this body I am not a goddess. I am as human as you are, with the same desires you have. I can experience pleasure and I enjoy it as much as any mortal woman."

Stepping closer, she pressed her nude body against his. She felt warm and soft and yielding.

Viran reacted to her touch, groaned when her soft fingers curled around his erection. She pulled him down on top of her. Her thighs opened wide and her hand guided him gently. He moaned as his hard rod slipped easily into her welcoming channel. The soft walls of her vagina molded themselves tightly around his mast. She kissed him. He drank hungrily from her saliva and let the sweet nectar run down his throat. Waves of pleasure pulsed through his body as he pumped his pelvis between her clutching thighs.

She looked into his face with her green eyes wide open, her expression gentle and full of love. Her breath caught in her throat as she experienced her first orgasm.

Viran did not know if it was real or just an act, but he didn't care. His own climax approached and with a deep cry he erupted inside her.

She pushed gently against his chest, made him lie on his back and straddled him. With sinuous movements she writhed above him, her eyes locked with his. He put his hands over her bobbing breasts, kneaded them gently with strong fingers. Her hips snapped back and forth with ever increasing speed. "Come inside me…now!" she hissed, clamping down hard. He felt her discharge as he emptied his own into her.

Her mind slammed into his with the force of a tidal wave, melded with his. He saw himself through her eyes, saw the almost agonized expression on his face, felt the pulsing and gushing of his penis inside the cavity of her sex-organ, felt what she felt. He reached a level of pleasure unlike anything he ever experienced before.

She laughed inside his mind. "No mortal woman can ever give you this," she whispered soundlessly. "This is where I am different."

When she withdrew he felt sadness. How could a mere mortal woman match the passion of the Xandra? Would he ever be able to find satisfaction with a human woman?

"As I told you before, Viran, you will," the Xandra said, reading his mind. She wiggled her bottom, with him still lodged deeply inside her. "This any woman can give you, if she has some skills."

"It is not the same." Viran pulled her against him, twisted until he ended up on top of her. With forceful thrusts he began moving again. The Xandra laughed, wrapped her long legs around his torso, pushed against him. They moved thus for a long time. When Viran came inside her, she touched his mind again, more gently this time.

After that they lay on their backs, staring into the darkening sky, like two lovers. The Xandra was the first to move. Sitting up, she said, "I never finished telling you everything I wanted you to know."

"There is nothing I desire to know right now," Viran murmured.

"Aren't you curious why I want to have so many of your offspring?"

"The question has occurred to me." He turned onto his side, studied the shape of her breast. "You are so perfect," he commented and reached up to cup her breast.

She smiled and said, "I chose this form because human males find it attractive. I am a construct, but you, you are the product of genes and your environment. Your body developed like this naturally. That is why I wanted your seeds to grow inside my seed-pouches. Your sons will have your body."

"Will they all look like me?" Viran asked.

She shook strands of long red hair out of her face. "Each will have a different face, different color of hair. Some may even have beards."

"I thought Xandra-born could not have facial hair."

The Xandra laughed. "Only because I designed them so. That will also change."

Viran took his hand from her breast, rose to his feet. "Why do you need so many replicas of me?" he asked quietly.

She looked up at him, her expression solemn, her green eyes dark. "I am building an army, Viran, and you will be my General."

Before Viran could comment he heard the fluttering sound of large wings. Looking into the sky he watched the winged figure descent swiftly and land a shot distance away.

"Angela," the Xandra said, rising to her feet.

Angela inclined her blond head. "You have summoned me, Great Mother?"

Viran studied the winged girl. She looked taller than he remembered from their first meeting, her body more muscular, and her breasts larger. She was not the fragile, gentle angel she had been before her change. He had tasted her savage passion, and he knew of her voracious sexual appetite.

But her face looked still the same, beautiful and soft, like that of an innocent young virgin, except for her eyes. They burned with a deep, hot blue fire.

She saw Viran's look, saw him stare at her sex-organ.

"You desire me?" she asked. "Even though you just lay with the Xandra?" A dark shadow crossed her lovely face. "I am ready for you. I am always ready. You were right, Viran. It may have been a dubious gift."

The laughter of the Xandra rang through the small glade. "I gave you what you craved so much, daughter."

"I know, but must it always be like this?" Angela touched her nipples, they were rigid, swollen. Then she cupped her mound. "I cannot be satisfied," she whispered, a pleading look in her eyes.

"It will pass," the Xandra promised, "this is just a temporary phase of adjustment you are experiencing."

"Let it end, now." Angela begged. She knelt in front of the Xandra, her wings half-spread. "I am not happy, Great Mother."

The Xandra put a hand on the girl's head. "I did not design you to be happy, daughter. There will always be a certain amount of desire inside you. It must be so, or else you would not be able to do the things I want you to do. But you shall find satisfaction." She smiled. "There is always a trade-off. To know pleasure you must know pain." The Xandra turned to Viran. "Give her what she craves."

Viran nodded, walked over to Angela, took her hand and lifted her up. The winged girl heaved a deep sigh. Then she pushed Viran onto his back and straddled him. Viran needed no coaxing, his penis stood erect below his hard-muscled belly. A soft cry escaped Angela's lips, as she impaled herself on his stiff organ. Snapping her pelvis back and forth, she rode him without restraint.

Beside them, the Xandra stood, watching them for a moment. Then she turned and walked back to the village.

She smiled when Viran called out hoarsely, as he gave in to Angela's furious demands.

* * * *

Read the conclusion in Book Three, The Xandra, Goddess of Life